DEAD AMONG US

FRANK ROBERTSON

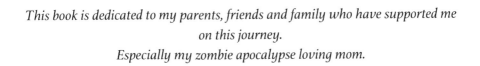

This book is dedicated to my parents, friends and family who have supported me on this journey.
Especially my zombie apocalypse loving mom.

1

As Garret had expected, the shelves were empty. Three dry liquor stores in a week. It was bad luck or rural America coveted their booze. Garret watched as his companion's face turned to stone.

When they first entered the store, the Irishman's eyes were bright with hope. But as he rifled through the looted store, his cheerful attitude evaporated. Despite knowing that the store was empty, the Irishman continued to check each shelf. Garret hoped they would find at least one bottle to placate the stubborn brute.

"You won't make it appear out of thin air," Garret said.

Broken shards of glass crunched under the Irishman's boots as he made his way to the back of the tiny store.

Garret turned towards Maps, who stood outside on watch as usual, soaking in the blazing summer sun, reading a newspaper he'd pulled from a vending machine. Garret tried to motion him inside, hoping he'd help diffuse the lit powder keg that was about to go off. Just when Garret thought he grabbed the stickman's attention, Maps looked back down into the newspaper, uninterested in intervening.

"Goddamned alcoholic small-town, hick fucks," the Irishman ranted.

"Let's go. There's a grocery store down the road we can hit. Might get lucky over there," Garret said.

The Irishman slammed his hand down on the counter.

"Keep it down, man," Garret said.

"This whole fucking town is dry."

"How about this?" Garret held up a bottle of expired Margarita mix.

The Irishman swept up the cash register in his arms and launched it through the front store window. Garret cringed at the noise of the window shattering.

"It was just a joke. Lighten up. Do you really need to drink tonight? And they're going to hear us if you keep making noise," Garret said and shuddered at the thought of the dead descending upon them.

"Fuck off," the Irishman spat.

And with that, five corpses turned the corner of Walnut Avenue. They were two blocks down the street, but Garret could already hear their obnoxious moans. He was almost certain their cries would draw more of the lifeless beings.

Maps acknowledged their presence with the sound of a sharp blade sliding out of its sheath.

"Great job! I'm surprised you didn't alert more."

The Irishman ignored Garret and stepped through the broken window, out into the street. "Hey, you fuckers, come get me. Brains, plenty of fresh brains, right here," the Irishman shouted. Without an ounce of fear he slid his blood stained brass knuckles over his right hand and thumped his chest with his left, bolstering himself before the battle.

Maps sheathed his K-bar knife and returned to reading the three-month-old newspaper.

"You going to help?" Garret asked, but Maps pretended not to hear him.

The five zombies shambled down the street with their eyes glued on the three humans. A raucous of growls and pained moans filled the air. The Irishman barreled toward them, Garret followed behind as backup, keeping his hand on the tool belt wrapped around his waist.

A former priest led the charge before he tripped on its own tattered robes and crashed into the street. An unfortunate fall landed him near the Irishman's boots. The Irishman stomped the creature's head into the curb, silencing its wretched moans. The sickening crunch echoed down the street as a warning to those that followed.

A short, chubby zombie missing the lower half of its jaw was next. The Irishman threw a vicious right hook. His brass knuckles caved in the corpse's forehead, causing the monster to fall backwards into the group. The Irishman followed through with three lightning fast punches, dealing out death to the remaining zombies. He brushed the gory brass knuckles off on his jeans.

"No problem here, mate. Don't get so bent out of shape over five of 'em." He patted Garret on the back and continued down the street towards the grocery store.

Garret looked down at the mess the Irishman left in his wake. Chipped bone fragments and rotten flesh lay at his feet. Three months ago the sight would have made Garret puke. Now it was normal. Garret stared into the puddle of gore.

When reality first warped into this hellish nightmare, Garret had been on a business trip, staying at a hotel in Miami over one thousand miles away from home. For a week he stayed holed up in his hotel room. He watched the world spiral out of control on T.V. During the first few days, news stations went back and forth, trying to decipher what happened. At first the media labeled it as a pandemic and then a bio-terrorist attack. But Garret got the sense that nobody knew the truth.

Then the broadcasts stopped. Chaos unfolded around him. Outside of his room on the 20th floor, the city buzzed with panic, sirens and screams. So he waited, hoping it would blow over. Slowly man made noise faded away, day by day as the dead overwhelmed the city. The help he expected never came.

Garret survived off of trail mix, candy bars and a random assortment of snacks for two weeks. The hotel lost power and running water after that, leaving Garret in darkness. Even then Garret stayed huddled in his hotel room, gripped by fear. He'd rather die from starvation than risk getting torn to pieces by a mob of corpses. After several days of drinking out of the toilet tank, Garret worked up enough courage to leave.

His survival instincts always urged him to run. When it boiled down to fight-or-flight, Garret always chose the latter. So he ran as they chased him down 26 flights of stairs. Garret still had nightmares about that day. Their arms lashed out, dirty fingernails nipping at his back. Just run, he thought.

With a bit of luck, he escaped from the hotel. Though the streets of Miami weren't much safer. Thankfully, Garret ran into Maps and the Irishman. Two embodiments of fight. Exactly what he needed to stand a chance to get home. He knew if he hadn't met them, he would have died there. Either torn to bits by the dead or murdered by those that lost their humanity.

Garret's stomach rumbled, snapping him back to reality. Maybe they'd get lucky and find some beer to placate the alcoholic.

"I need a fucking drink, let's get moving," the Irishman said.

Maps finished reading the newspaper and dropped it to the ground, letting the wind carry it off into the road.

Albert's Grocery was looted except for two cans of carrots that had rolled underneath a shelf. Countless bodies littered the rest of the store.

Garret counted over twenty decomposing corpses as they walked the aisles, all of which were picked down to the bone. Bloody footprints caked the tiled floor. Rancid meat and the smell of death wafted through the air, making Garret gag.

The noxious odor didn't stop the Irishman from popping a can of carrots open and dumping half of the contents into his mouth. He titled the can towards Maps, offering him a portion, but the thin man declined. The Irishman ignored Garret and continued devouring his meal. Carrot juice slid down the side of his grizzled face.

Garret didn't mind the Irishman's slight. He would rather have the brute not share food than cause anymore commotion. Plus, he hated carrots. They used to have two backpacks filled with canned goods and granola bars, but those supplies had dwindled. They had maybe a week's worth of food if they stretched it. Garret had been saving a chewy peanut butter bar for when he was really starving.

Maps only ate when necessary. His skinny build reflected his dislike of canned foods. The Irishman, on the other-hand ate like a mule. Garret refused to let him carry the food supply backpack. Instead, they made him carry a bag of other equipment.

"Are we setting up camp?" the Irishman asked Maps. Maps turned to Garret and shrugged.

"No, we can cover at least two more miles. Put some distance between us and Greensville."

The Irishman spat on the ground, obviously not interested in more walking. They had already covered twenty miles, which was more than usual in one day.

Walking was how they spent most of their time. They often traversed through the woods on roundabout trails and back roads, avoiding major highways and dense population centers. When supplies dwindled, they dipped into low population areas to scavenge for food, booze, and meds. Maps had a clear talent for navigation and had yet to get them lost. Hence the nickname Garret had given him.

Garret traveled with the odd pair now for two months and still didn't know their names. When he asked the Irishman, the brute laughed and said, "We're all living on borrowed time. What's the point of getting to know someone when we're all one bad day away from death?"

When Garret asked Maps, the thin man just didn't respond. He didn't take it personally. The guy talked about as much as he smiled. Instead of pushing them, Garret gave up. He didn't care who they were as long as he made it home.

Garret recognized early on that he wasn't cut out for survival. No, he should've been dead several times over. And despite the pair saving his life multiple times in the previous weeks, Garret felt disposable. He imagined if he died the Irishman would say something like, "Rest in peace, dumbass."

He'd barely convinced the two survivors to even accompany him. Like a true salesman, Garret sold them on an idea by weaving a tale of his fortress in Pennsylvania. A fortress that contained a massive collection of expensive liquor Garret stocked over the years, and a bunker filled to the brim with MREs and supplies.

Garret remembered telling his wife that a bomb shelter was a silly idea. In fact, for months the topic was a launch board for arguments. If he ever got the chance to see her again, he'd admit he was wrong. Actually, he'd kill to hear her say, "I told you so," one more time.

"Bunch of damn drunks in this town," the Irishman complained.

"They can't be worse than you. I'd be your sponsor if I wasn't sure you'd kill me," Garret said.

"Shut up. These bastards didn't leave one drop of booze in this place. I hope they fucking choke on it. Hell, I'd even drink some wine at this point."

"Maybe we'll find some in the next town."

"Forget it, let's get out of this shit hole," the Irishman said as he finished his canned carrots.

As they prepared for departure, Garret heard a rustling in the back, mixed with faint cries of agony. Garret stood up, his fingernails bit into the head of his hammer.

"Yeah, let's get moving." He shuddered.

2

GREENSVILLE RESEMBLED the dozen other ghost towns they'd traveled through before it. The dead picked the rural town clean and moved on, leaving it void of life. Only a few stragglers remained.

A long sigh escaped Garret's mouth as the blistering sun beat on the back of his neck. These long walks in the sweltering heat made Garret's clothes stick to his body as if he'd jumped into a pool. He wished they would just hot-wire another vehicle and take their chances on the road. Traveling by car had its pros, but also many cons. Risks heavily outweighed the reward. Especially when compared to moving by foot. The noise of a rumbling engine attracted both the dead and living alike. Wrecked vehicles and sometimes hordes of the dead blocked the highways, making extended drives difficult if not downright impossible. They could run over a pack of twenty zombies, but hundreds was another story.

Less than a month ago they covered a good amount of ground in a brand new jeep they'd stolen off a car lot in North Carolina. The blisters on their feet convinced them to give driving another chance. The Irishman bitched the entire time. Garret convinced him with the idea that they could much more efficiently track down booze for his insatiable craving. They didn't make it over twenty miles before they got trapped on the interstate, pinned between two writhing armies of rotten flesh. The event resulted in them exhausting the rest of their ammo and abandoning their jeep. Over the next forty hours they moved by foot, putting distance between themselves and the dead. Most of the corpses moved at a snail's pace, but they were persistent. Eventually they lost the slow, plodding mass of death. Since then they opted for the safer but slower option of traveling by foot.

"Double cheeseburger, with extra bacon, grilled onions and raw onions, fresh jalapeños, ketchup, mustard, mayo, fuck I'd even take a tomato and some lettuce, with a soft potato bun," the Irishman said.

The thought made Garret's mouth water. Half of him hated this game, but the other half loved entertaining the idea of eating a proper meal. He doubted he'd ever enjoy the luxury of biting into a fresh, juicy burger again.

"I want some greasy Chinese food from a hole in the wall joint, with crab rangoon. You know, the ones with the fake crab meat and too much cream cheese. Throw in two or three egg rolls, some pot stickers and a bowl of fried rice with some Szechuan chicken," Garret said.

Maps said nothing, as usual. Garret wondered what kind of food the stick man consumed before the world ended. From his lean, bony build, Garret assumed he ate nothing but salads, fruits, and nuts.

"Maps, what about you?" Garret asked.

"Uh, a ham sandwich."

The Irishman kicked an empty soda can out of the street. "Way to use your imagination, buddy."

They walked a mile and a half north, entertaining the thought of setting up camp for the night. As they reached the outer edge of Greensville, the Irishman pointed to a church sitting atop a hill.

Garret shook his head. "No, thanks. Let's just keep walking until we find a house to hunker down in." But it was too late. The Irishman ignored Garret and started up the hill.

"That's fine. Me and Maps are leaving you, enjoy that creepy church."

Maps brushed past Garret following the Irishman's lead.

"You too? Fine..."

The church looked more like a barn with a big cross posted above its front doors. The fading sun cast the church's shadow down the hill. Garret welcomed the refreshing coolness as he stepped into the shade. Maps and the Irishman waited for Garret in the modest parking lot at the top of the plateau.

Worn wooden boards held the small house of worship together. A cross colored by chipped and faded white paint rested under the gable. It looked like a small gust of wind could send the whole building crashing down.

"Why are you so set on staying in this dump? We still got an hour of sunlight left," Garret said.

Neither Maps nor the Irishman bothered with answering Garret's question. Instead, they approached the front of the church with caution, not wanting to make any noise. Garret heaved a deep sigh and walked toward them. His muscles ached with each step.

The Irishman stood outside of a grime covered stained glass window. He spit on the pane of glass and rubbed away the grit with the bottom of his shirt. He cupped his hands around his eyes and pressed them to the window.

"See anything?"

"Yeah, don't you smell them?" the Irishman asked.

Garret didn't notice any particularly foul scent besides the usual sweat and musk from not having a hot shower in three months. The closest thing he had to a shower was a quick sponge bath in a river last week.

"Shit, there's a dozen in there," the Irishman said.

"Good, let's forget about it then."

The Irishman remained unswayed. Garret rested his hand on the hammer hanging from his tool belt. Maps unsheathed his knife.

The Irishman turned to Garret. "It's your turn to be bait."

"To hell with that. I'm always bait. I was bait the last five times -- no, six times actually," Garret said.

"You're really keeping count? Being the bait is the easiest role. Just open the door and lead those fuckers out. Maps and I will swoop in from behind and brain the bastards," the Irishman said.

"Fine."

Exhausted from all the walking, Garret couldn't muster the resolve needed to argue with the brute. Not that there were any words in the entire English language that could persuade the Irishman to change his mind. Stubborn bastard.

Maps and The Irishman disappeared behind the side of the church, waiting for Garret to execute the plan. Garret's mouth went dry as he approached the front entrance. Anxiety ran up his spine like a swarm of cockroaches exposed to light. He pulled the hammer from his belt and tightened his grip around the rubber handle. His pulse quickened. Dry moaning sounds escaped underneath the door. A rotten smell followed, sucker punching Garret's senses. Stomach acid shot up his throat.

Garret swung the door open. Light poured into the church, revealing a dozen pairs of lifeless eyes now fixated on him. "Uh, guys," Garret said and stumbled backwards. The corpses swarmed forward in unison like a wave crashing over a beach.

Two lanky teenagers in tattered dress clothes led the charge. Their speed took Garret by surprise. He backed up into the parking lot, swinging his hammer wildly through the air. Through sheer panic, Garret wielded the blunt weapon, failing to hit the two zombies, strutting towards him. One teenager, ignorant of the gaping hole in its abdomen, its entrails dragging behind him, pushed forward and closed the gap.

"Holy shit!" Garret screamed.

The salesman swung again, barely clipping the front of the boy's nose. Fear overwhelmed Garret as the monster shrugged off the attack. Its nose hung from its face, dangling by a thread of colorless flesh.

"Get the hell back!" Garret yelled, retreating backwards.

Overwhelmed by the two zombies, Garret didn't notice the parking block inches behind him. The heel of Garret's boot caught the raised concrete, sending him tumbling back onto the asphalt. The Irishman's words rushed back through Garret's head. "Don't let them get you on the ground. Fall down and you're finished."

The teenagers lurched forward, throwing themselves at Garret. Their bodies crashed into him, knocking him over,pressing Garret to the ground. He bucked desperately against the corpses as their foul breath stung his eyes, unable to move with the weight of the two bodies stacked on top of him. Fingernails dug into his right shoulder. The creature's head jerked forward, its teeth barely missing his cheek.Garret wedged the hammer into the teenager's mouth.

"Jesus Christ, someone get them off me!" Garret yelled, twisting the hammer, scraping the metal against the creature's enamel. Garret jammed the hammer further into its mouth, using all of his force. Teeth snapped as he thrust the tool into the back of the creature's throat. The second teenager climbed over its brother, intent on sinking its teeth into Garret's flesh.

This was it. Pinned by two corpses with his weapon stuck. It all ended here. He tried to roll out from under them, but their combined weight made it impossible.At that moment, Garret thought of Emily. Random images of their wedding day flashed through his head. He stared into the monster's gaping maw as it prepared to sink its teeth into his face.

A serrated blade burst forward through the back of the creature's head. The tip of the knife stopped less than an inch from Garret's nose.

Maps pulled the knife out and rolled the corpse to the side. Seizing the opening, Garret rolled away from the one with the hammer still lodged in its throat. He scrambled to his feet and watched Maps dispose of the remaining zombie with his blade. The thin man yanked the hammer from the corpse's mouth, pulling out strips of its throat.Maps casually tossed the weapon at Garret's feet, like he'd recovered his friend's lost golf ball.

His panic subsiding, Garret looked toward the church where the Irishman towered over the pile of freshly brained church-goers. Their eyes met, and the Irishman shook his head in embarrassment. Garret felt like he was seventeen again and just failed his driving test because he couldn't parallel park. Maps patted him on the back in consolation, like he was saying, "Don't worry, not everyone has a knack for survival."

They walked into the rickety church in silence.

The Irishman tore through the church like he was a crackhead looking for a misplaced rock. Eventually, he found two bottles of communion wine tucked away in a closet behind the stage. Within five minutes, the Irishman drained two-thirds of the first bottle. It finally dawned on Garret why the Irishman had been dead-set on clearing the church.

Garret peeled back the plastic from a processed meat stick and took a bite. He didn't particularly care for the cajun jerk flavor two weeks ago, but now it tasted like a beautiful medium-rare Wagyu steak. He laid his head back on the wooden pew and stared at the ceiling, replaying the day's events in his head.

"Maps is taking the first watch," the Irishman said with a mouthful of kidney beans.

"We barricaded the doors, is that really necessary?" Garret asked.

The Irishman took a long swig of communion wine. He wiped a mix of bean juice and alcohol from his chin and asked, "Do you like being alive?"

Garret immediately regretted his question. He knew the Irishman always answered what he deemed as stupid questions with an even dumber question. It pissed Garret off.

"No, being alive sucks," Garret said, knowing his sarcasm would piss off the Irishman in return.

"I can help you with that smart ass." The Irishman chucked the empty can of beans at Garret.

Garret slapped the tin can out of the air. "Asshole."

"Dumbass." The Irishman sprang up from his relaxed posture and leaned forward in the pew across from Garret.

Garret knew a lecture, story, or a hypothetical situation was about to come out of the drunk's mouth. He felt the Irishman's judgmental gaze wash over him, as if he were a mere boy again, about to be scowled by his teacher.

"OK, smart guy." The Irishman took another sip from the bottle and continued, "Say a priest shows up tonight."

"A priest?"

"Yeah, tonight a priest shows up at his church while we are all sleeping. He tries to open the door, but as you pointed out, it is well barricaded."

"OK, so?"

"So, he looks through one of these ugly stained glass windows and sees that we drank all the wine, ate all the communion wafers and trashed the place." The Irishman chucked the empty bottle of communion wine at the wooden podium. The bottle shattered. "And we're asleep, remember? Cause you don't want to keep watch. So he sets the place ablaze."

Garret laughed. "The priest sets his own church on fire? I'm pretty sure we killed all the parishioners anyway, well... You guys did."

"Guess you didn't get the notice that the fucking world has ended Garret, everyone's lost their shit. Anyway, the entire building is burning. You die from smoke inhalation because nobody is on watch. Maps wakes up just in time and we jump through one of these ugly, stained glass windows. Maps slices an artery and bleeds out in 90 seconds. I make it out with a few scratches. I'm ready to slay this bastard priest for killing you guys, but it's not just the priest. It's his entire congregation and they tear me apart with pitchforks." The Irishman finished his story and laid back on his pew.

"Thanks for letting me die peacefully, I guess."

Garret finished his beef stick and laid back down on the cushioned pew. Yes, many people had gone crazy, he admitted. Societal collapse didn't bring the best out of people. In fact, Garret had been saved from the very type of deranged individuals in the Irishman's story.

"Second or third watch?" the Irishman asked.

"Second, I guess."

The Irishman sighed.

"What?"

"I don't think you get it. The difference between you and us is that we survive. Every day, we push forward, accepting the risks of this new world. We deal with it, without thinking. Like earlier today when you froze up."

"I didn't freeze up," Garret said.

The Irishman laughed. "You let panic take control. You swung that fucking hammer like you were doing some kind of interpretive dance. We brained a dozen of those fuckers while you got overwhelmed by two kids. It's a literal miracle that you haven't died yet."

"So, I'm not great in combat. Sorry," Garret said.

"That's not it." The Irishman eyed the second bottle of communion wine, calculating whether to dip into it before he continued. "You were looking at those boys as if they still had a shred of humanity. Like you didn't want to kill them. You hesitated, panicked, and almost died. Don't you want to see your wife again? What's her fucking name, Emma-Emmy something?"

"Her name is Emily, and she's the only thing keeping me going," Garret said, letting the anger peak in his voice.

The Irishman shook his head. "You're going to run out of luck and die if you don't pull your head out of your ass. Don't let fear hold you back, cause the second you freeze you're dead. Next time one of those bastards is coming for you, I want to see you bash its fucking brains in. You understand me?"

"Yeah," Garret said and rolled over, turning his back to the Irishman as he tried to fall asleep.

Minutes felt like hours as Garret tried to get comfortable, shifting his weight on the pew. But the earlier brush with death and the Irishman's lecture left his mind restless. Just as he was about to fall asleep, Maps tapped him on the shoulder. Without saying a word, Garret sat up and started his watch.

3

THE THREE SURVIVORS headed East into the forest north of Greensville. They followed Buck Creek, moving parallel to Highway 40. They refilled their canteens and four plastic bottles of water from a nearby stream before continuing on the hike.

Maps moved faster than Garret or the Irishman. It was common for him to scout a few hundred yards ahead, keeping an eye out for any wildlife. Their guns had run dry long ago and they didn't have luck to find more ammo. Maps carried nothing but a K-bar knife and an empty Glock 19 that he kept tucked in his inner waistband holster. Though he didn't need a gun to hunt. Garret witnessed Maps sneak up on a rabbit and snap its neck before it even knew he was there.

"Shit, we can't keep up with em," the Irishman said, breathing heavily.

"I don't think he's expecting us to," Garret said.

"Good." The Irishman sat down on a stump. He opened his backpack and pulled out his prized humidor. In a flash, he lit the cigar with a match and took a big puff. He slapped at a mosquito as he stoked the tiny ember. A cloud of tobacco smoke billowed out of his mouth.

Garret posted up against a tree and tapped his foot. He didn't want Maps to put too much distance between them. The Irishman took a third puff before putting out the cigar. He packed it away in the black humidor and they continued their trek through the forest.

They hiked up a hill, giving them clear sight over a stretch of the highway. Broken-down cars, eighteen wheelers, pickup-trucks and a burned out overturned sedan were strewn across the road. Five hundred yards to the north, the tree line gave way to open fields. In the heart of the wreckage, an eighteen wheeler blocked both sides of the road.

A deceased family of four ambled down the road in the distance. In some way the sight relieved Garret. Sometimes they went days without encountering the dead. Despite his companions, the world felt hopelessly desolate, and that disturbed Garret more than a handful of zombies. The 150 yard distance between the corpses also helped put him at ease. At least for now, they could avoid the close quarters combat Garret dreaded.

"I don't see Maps," Garret said.

"Eh, don't worry your little heart about him. He's around," the Irishman grunted. "I'm feeling lucky. Let's kill this lot and loot a few of these cars."

Before Garret could protest, the Irishman started down the hill toward the road through a thorny patch of brush. Trying not to lose his footing on the sloped terrain, Garret followed moving with care. Twisting his ankle would be a death sentence. There wasn't a doubt in his mind that the Irishman would leave him behind. He could already hear the brute saying something like, "You expect me to carry your sniveling ass?" In such an event, maybe Maps would slow the pace down. Even then, that wasn't a sure bet. Maps had said less than three dozen words over the past two months. Garret read people for a living, yet the thin man eluded him.

"Wait up," Garret said as he pushed through the brush reaching the base of the hill, walking toward the embankment. He kept his head on a swivel, paranoid that a straggling corpse would appear from nowhere and tear into his flesh.

After crossing onto the road, Garret spotted the Irishman a few yards ahead of him, barreling toward the wrecked vehicles. A farmer missing the flesh from his face in torn overalls snapped its head up and snarled in Garret's direction. What had once been a housewife stood by his side. Two children in torn, blood-soaked clothing and a cold hunger in their eyes scuffled behind them.

Garret readied his brick hammer and walked up the roadway behind the Irishman. Ahead of them, several wrecked vehicles blocked off most of the highway. Together they waited for the farmer and his family to funnel through the gap.

The monster scraped its grey flesh on the front of an old Buick as it forced itself toward its potential meal. The Irishman wound back his arm, waiting for the target to walk mindlessly into his range. But the farmer stopped inches outside of the Irishman's reach. The Irishman stood in shock as the housewife leap frogged over the farmer, tackling him to the asphalt. The Irishman lay on his back with his hands wrapped around the dead woman's throat.

"Get this bitch off me!"

Garret swung the brick hammer with precision, knowing if he clipped the Irishman, he may as well just let the zombies disembowel him. Thankfully, his strike connected, shattering the side of the corpse's head. Chipped pieces of bone rained over the Irishman as he pushed the now dead weight to the side.

"Watch out!" the Irishman spat.

The farmer lunged forward, grabbing at Garret, who shuffled backward. But it was too late. The creature's putrid fingernails sunk into his forearm, carving into Garret's flesh like it was malleable wax. Garret yelled as he swung the hammer into the side of the corpse's head. The impact rattled the monster. It lost balance and crashed into the asphalt, landing on its back. Ignoring the warm crimson flowing out of the cuts on his arm, Garret stumbled forward. Unfortunately, the adrenaline only suffocated half of the pain.

Garret jumped onto the zombie's chest, pinning it to the ground and swung the hammer in an effortless arc, the way the pendulum of a clock sways in perfect harmonic oscillation. The impact made Garret grit his teeth, and the sick crunching noise that followed made his stomach sour.

A horrible screech pierced through the air. Garret dropped his hammer and threw his hands up covering his ears. A pig tailed zombie girl wailed next to her pint-sized brother. The Irishman slid across the hood of the Buick and silenced the noise. Only the small boy remained. Garret turned away while the Irishman finished his work. He wiped the slick flesh from his brass knuckles onto his jeans. A thin trail of blood leaked from his right ear.

The Irishman sighed and let out a single, "Fuck."

"When did they start screaming like that?" Garret asked.

"Never seen em jump like that before either."

Garret turned his head from the dead children lying broken in the street, heartbroken from the sight. A nauseous wave rolled over Garret. His stomach gurgled.

"Come on now Garret, they aren't kids anymore. They were little monsters that needed someone to kill them. Trust me, I don't get my rocks off from this shit. Damn, looks like farmer Bill got your arm good. Like he had metal fingernails," the Irishman said as he smashed a window out of the Buick and began rummaging through it.

Pain surged through Garret. He winced as he inspected his wound. It looked like someone had dragged a cheese grater down his forearm.

"Hey, I'm bleeding a lot," Garret said, attempting to hide the creeping panic in his voice.

"Stop crying, it's just a scratch," the Irishman spat as he pillaged the car.

A minute later, the Irishman popped the trunk and produced a first aid kit with a shit-eating grin on his face. He tossed Garret a roll of bandages, some tape, and antiseptic. Garret applied the antiseptic ointment, wrapped a layer of bandage over the scrape, and taped it tight.

"Nothing worthwhile in here, bunch of junk," the Irishman said.

"Shit."

"Where the fuck did Maps go?" the Irishman asked.

"You said he was around."

The roar of an engine cut through the air. Garret turned to see a red pickup truck flying towards him and the Irishman. Sandwiched between an eighteen wheeler and the pickup, they had nowhere to run.

The truck parked about ten yards away from them, next to a brown convertible, the highway wreckage prevented the vehicle's advance. A man stood in the pickup's bed with a shotgun. He was wearing a pair of jeans and a dirty sheriff's department uniform. A dirt smudged badge hung off his belt. The driver had a sunburned face and a smile showing a mouthful of crooked teeth.He looked far from police material. Sunburn climbed out of the truck with a tire iron.

The deputy pointed the shotgun at Garret. "Take that backpack off and throw it over here. Do it slowly,"

Garret slid the backpack off, making eye contact with the Irishman.

"Don't look at him, look at me."

"How bout you two fuck off and we won't kill ya," the Irishman said.

The deputy turned the shotgun to the Irishman. "You too. Throw the backpack off and put your hands behind your back!" he shouted.

The Irishman and Garret tossed their backpacks towards the pickup. Sunburn snatched them off the ground. He unzipped Garret's backpack and peeked inside. The contents made him smile.

"Got some food here, boss." His grin widened, showing off his crooked teeth. The deputy in the back of the truck took one hand off his shotgun and grabbed the radio off his belt.

"Reed, nice catch. You can move in," the deputy said over the radio.

"What now? You going to kill us, police officer?" the Irishman asked.

The deputy ignored him and clicked his radio. "Reed, copy that?"

No response.

"Reed, copy?" the deputy asked again.

The Irishman lowered his hands as the man with crooked teeth rummaged through his backpack. He found the humidor and pulled it out. The Irishman took a step towards him.

"You shouldn't touch shit that isn't yours," the Irishman said.

The ugly, sunburned man's gaze turned to the towering brute.

The deputy put his hand back on the shotgun and leveled it at the Irishman. "Don't fucking move. Mike cuff them. The big guy first. Hit him in the head if he resists. No need to waste the bullets."

The deputy grabbed two pairs of handcuffs from his belt and tossed them to Mike. "Get on your knees, hands behind your back!" the deputy shouted. He clicked the radio, "Reed, come in. Over."

The Irishman slowly put his hands behind his head, but refused to kneel. Garret's heart raced. He was ready to dive into Mike or make a run for it. Garret was fast, years of highschool track made sure of that, but he didn't want to outrun gunfire.

Mike stepped toward the Irishman, carrying the hand-cuffs and gripping the tire iron with devious intent.

Garret was ready to make his move when a glint of reflected light caught his eyes. He searched for the source and found it. Maps lay on his belly underneath a car a few yards from the red pickup. He held his K-bar knife in one hand and a shard of glass in the other. He twisted the shard, beaming the sunlight across the Irishman's face.

"Get on your fucking knees!" the deputy yelled louder. His finger tightened on the trigger.

The Irishman grinned at Garret.

"Don't smile at him, boy," Mike said.

The Irishman submitted to one knee. Mike took another step towards him.

Garret made his move. He dashed to the left, away from The Irishman, hoping to draw fire. A shotgun blast boomed through the sky. Garret landed hard on the ground behind a busted convertible. Hot pain seared through his body.

Before the deputy could chamber another round in his shotgun, Maps rolled out from under the convertible, leapt into the back of the pickup, and stabbed the deputy deep in his chest with his serrated blade. The deputy cried out in a horrifying combination of shock and pain, looking down as Maps sawed into him. He dragged the knife through his sternum and twisted it in his guts, shredding his intestines, before pulling the blade out.

Mike swung his tire iron, and the Irishman dodged. He took another swing, and the Irishman evaded to the side, seemingly bored with their dance. Mike turned around to the screams of his boss being gutted like a deer. He watched in horror as the deputy's guts spilled out into the bed of the truck.

They outnumbered him. Mike stumbled backwards. He realized there was nowhere to run and dropped the tire iron, pinned between the Irishman and Maps. He dropped to his knees and threw his hands into the air.

"Please don't hurt me. None of this was my idea. We are just hungry you got to understand," he pleaded.

The Irishman snapped his brass knuckle laced fist into the man's jaw, breaking his crooked teeth and destroying the lower half of the desperate fellow's mouth.

Mike crashed onto his back, choking on his blood. He turned his head to the side and spit shattered enamel and mucus across the asphalt. The man couldn't speak, but he begged for his life with his eyes and threw his right hand up in defense.

"I told you before. You don't take shit that doesn't belong to you," the Irishman said and wound back his fist, ready to end the pitiful man's life.

"Stop it," Garret said as he leaned against the convertible. He gripped his side, which had caught a few pellets from the shotgun. The wound stung as fresh blood trickled through his fingers. A dizzying sensation fluttered through his head, like he had spun around in his office chair too fast.

"I'm not leaving this piece of trash alive," said The Irishman.

Tears streamed down the man's sunburned cheeks as he tried to hold his broken face together with his left hand. The Irishman's single punch had left Mike's nose and cheekbones shattered.

"Leave the bastard alone. He probably won't survive the night anyway," Garret said.

Instead of crushing the man's skull with the heel of his boot, the Irishman pulled Mike off the pavement by his collar, tearing his shirt. "If I see you again, I'll kill you twice," the Irishman said, spat in his face and pushed him off the highway. Mike took his second chance at life and ran with it into the woods.

Maps rushed to assist Garret. With care, Garret slid his shirt up over the wound. Blood oozed out of three tiny holes to the left of his belly button. The nasty bite of buckshot had torn open his flesh.

"Am I going to die?" Garret asked.

"No," Maps said.

"Maps if you ever pull that shit again," the Irishman held up his brass knuckle laced fist and scooped his humidor into his backpack.

"He saved our asses," Garret said.

"No. He used us as fucking bait, you dumb clown," the Irishman said. His eyes bore into Maps. "You waited for their spotter to call us in, and then you snaked up behind him and slit his throat. Didn't you?"

Maps ignored him and helped Garret into the back of the red pickup.

"Shut up for five minutes. None of this should have happened. You're the one that had to loot these damned cars, probably looking for more booze," Garret said as Maps treated him with the first aid kit.

"None of this? Are you stupid? Now we have guns and a truck. Oh, you got shot. Sorry mate. Forgot about that one, but you'll be fine, really. Let's drive a couple days, aren't we all fucking tired of walking?" the Irishman asked.

Garret put a bloody hand to his head in frustration.

"Keep pressure," Maps said to Garret as he leaned over the deputy's body, relieving him of his equipment belt.

Garret put pressure on his damaged flesh, but it burned too hot. He sunk back against the spare tire. The Irishman handed him a clean handkerchief through the rear window as he leaned into the driver's seat.

"There are so few living people left in this world," Garret said.

The Irishman paused. "Don't give me your morality shit. They were probably fucking cannibals. Ha, well at least that guy won't be eating red meat soon." The Irishman laughed at his own joke.

Garret shook his head, tired of the callous remarks.

"Brain that bastard before he gets back up." The Irishman pointed to the deputy.

"Oh no, he's still alive?" Garret looked down at the poor bastard laying in the truck's bed and then at his own injury. The deputy was no longer making much noise. Just quick, strained breaths. His eyes remained unaware of the reaper standing over him. He just stared past him and into the cloudy sky. Maps rolled the deputy out of the truck.

"This is what it's about now." The Irishman held up a silver .38 Special he found in the glove-box.

"Guns?" Garret asked.

"No," the Irishman said. "Risk and reward."

Along with the revolver, The Irishman discovered a box of shotgun shells. He tossed the box back to Maps. Maps examined the Remington 12-Gauge pump action. He chambered a third slug into the shotgun, grabbed a handful of buckshot and slid them into his breast pocket.

Garret pressed the cloth to his wound. The pellet holes burned like fire. He had seen a hundred action films in his life and maybe even more medical procedural shows, but he never imagined that a gunshot wound would burn like someone kept sticking him with a hot poker. The bleeding seemed to slow, but he wondered how much blood he had already lost. A wave of light-headedness washed over him.

"You with me?" Maps asked.

"Yeah, I'm great," Garret said. He tried not to look down at the bloody handkerchief.

The C.B. radio clicked on in the center console. A deep voice crackled out of the radio, "1555 report in, over."

The Irishman revved the engine to life. He put his foot on the gas and turned the truck towards Miller road. "Half a tank left."

"10-37" the radio clicked again.

"1844 inbound on 1555's last known location."

"Ya hear that?" the Irishman asked.

Maps frowned. He wiped the drying blood from his knife on to his mud splattered jeans.

The trees became a blur as the Irishman shot the truck through the twisted countryside. The dark green foliage turned into a runny oil painting as they drove by.Garret savored the few moments of beauty and peace before being dragged back to their harsh reality.

Black clouds blocked the sun, cooling the blazing summer air. Maps stared off into the skyline at a trail of gray smoke. He tapped on the back window for the Irishman to slow down, but either he didn't hear it or ignored him. Maps tightened his grip on the side of the truck, uncomfortable with the Irishman's speed. The Irishman took a hard right thirty miles per hour too fast. Their vehicle jerked over a corpse in the road.

Maps banged on the back window and yelled, "Pull over!"

The Irishman flicked him off as they took another hard turn. He turned to Maps, knowingly keeping his eyes off the road.He could see the nerves jumping in Map's eyes. "I've never seen you this anxious before.Don't worry, bud. I've taken an offensive driving class!" the Irishman yelled through the back window, without slowing down.

"We should've never let you drive!" Garret said. His pain intensified with each turn.

The tree line gave way to open pastures. The road straightened out. Garret let out a deep breath and looked at a farmhouse in the distance. The Irishman whipped the truck around another bend. The road dipped, as did Garret's stomach. They passed by an abandoned bait shop and a barbeque restaurant with a smiling pig on the building.

Static came in over the C.B.

"This is 1844. The truck's gone and deputy Jordan is dead. Somebody cut him up real good. It's disgusting, Sheriff. No sign of Mike either. Reed ain't responding to the C.B."

"Eighteen forty-four stick to the goddamn codes. Hostile forces could be listening," the Sheriff said.

"I don't know the codes for this Sheriff."

"Deputy Lindell, take the comm away from that dipshit. Switch to the backup frequency."

"Roger that, Sheriff," deputy Lindell said.

The Irishman grabbed the radio mic and clicked on the transmit button. "Save yourself some bodies and turn the fuck around.I'll kill every bastard you send my way!" he yelled.

The road curved, forcing Maps and Garret to hold on for their lives.

"Code 2, 11-56. All units. Suspect last known location westbound on Miller Road. I repeat, all units are to pursue the suspects and change to the goddamn backup frequency."

"All units?" Garret shouted.

"It's the apocalypse. How many can that really be?" the Irishman yelled back.

"You talk too much!" Maps said.

"I gotta make up for your lack of conversation." The Irishman took his eyes off the twisted road for a moment too long.

Garret tried to warn him, but it was too late. The Irishman slammed on the brakes. Tires screeched as the front grill of the truck smashed into the poor man, throwing him into the air. He landed a dozen feet back onto the road. Canned goods rolled out of his cloth sack across the pavement.

4

"S HIT." The Irishman pulled the gear stick into park and looked back to see if his comrades were still in the pickup's bed. Maps was already standing up, pointing the shotgun toward the tree-line.

Garret grunted in pain as he clutched his bandaged forearm. "What the hell did he hit?" Garret asked, sitting up.

A woman's scream exploded from the woods, followed by a chubby blonde woman. She jogged out from behind a large oak tree, her arms flailed wildly, tears streaming down her face. She ran over to her boyfriend lying on the road.

He reached up to stroke the tears from her cheeks, but his mangled arm fell back to the ground. The woman turned to the trees and cried, "Jesus Christ, someone help!" She cradled his ragged head in her lap and begged him between panicked breaths, "David, baby please wake up."

Two men appeared from behind the wall of oak trees. The first man stood six foot three with a light brown, sun stained beard. He looked to be in his twenties. The shadow of him and his AR-15 extended across the pavement. He leaned into the rifle, aiming it at Maps. An older man trailed behind him out from the brush, clutching a revolver with shaky hands.

"Drop your guns." The tall man cast his words out from the forest.

"Yours first," the Irishman said as he leaned out of the passenger side window. The brute tightened his grip around the snub-nosed revolver, drawing a bead on the old man.

Garret sunk down in the pickup's bed, fear running rampant through his system. If bullets started flying, he hoped they wouldn't pierce through the side of the truck.

The old man crept slowly onto the road, pistol in hand pointed at the Irishman. "I don't want to shoot you, son, but I will if I have to." The old man turned to the blonde woman, sobbing over her dying lover.

Maps lowered his gun. The tall bearded man behind the oak tree followed suit. Finally, The Irishman tucked his newfound .38 away into his waistband.

"Stacy, sweetheart, we need to go now. David would have wanted you to pull through this. We have to keep moving," the old man said as he patted her on the back.

Through thick heaving sobs she stuttered, "I'm... Not... Leaving... Him..."

"Sweetie, he's gone. He wouldn't want you to see him turn into one of those things." The old man pulled her up from the road. He put his arm around her shoulder and pulled her away from the body.

The tall bearded man walked out from the tree line, still grasping the AR-15's pistol grip.

Garret leaned out of the side of the pickup's bed and examined the uneasy group. These people didn't seem like ruthless bandits. If they were, Garret was sure bullets would have already flown.

"I'm Garret," he said.

"Garret, your friend just killed my friend," the tall man said, his hand never leaving his rifle.

Stacy broke away from the old man and his attempt to console her. She ran to the passenger's side of the truck and slammed her fists against the window. As she reached for the door handle, the Irishman locked it with the press of a button.

"You son of a bitch." She paced back and forth. "You fucking killed him!" She cried and smeared the window with her boyfriend's blood.

The Irishman didn't pay her any attention. He just stared at the ragged body, failing to feel guilt or any sense of regret.

The old man pulled her away from the truck. She pushed him back and walked to the tall, bearded man. "You're going to let them get away with this, Cody?" she asked. She poked him in the chest with her stubby finger. "You two were fucking friends... And you won't do anything about it?"

"Stacy, please," Cody said.

"We didn't mean to hit him, I swear," Garret said.

Stacy turned her rage toward Garret. "Fuck you. You piece of shit!"

A moment after her outburst, Stacy slapped Cody across the face. He reeled back. Stacy tried to smack him again, but he caught her wrist.

"Let go of me," she said. He released her wrist, and she shoved past him in an unstable fury, not able to look any of them in the eyes as they did nothing to avenge her boyfriend's meaningless death. She wiped at the snot dripping down her face with the tattered sleeve of her shirt. She walked back to her boyfriend's fresh corpse.

The shotgun hung limp in his hands, but Maps eased his finger back to the trigger, ready to swing the barrel up and shower them with buckshot if needed.

Garret failed to think of anything to say. No amount of words could ease the tension hanging in the air. Yet his mind raced, wanting to defuse the situation.

"Cody." A girl that couldn't be older than sixteen stepped out from the brush.

"Alyssa, I told you to stay down."

"I know, but I hear a lot of them coming." Alyssa pointed toward the forest.

Garret recognized the exhaustion in their eyes. "Listen," he said, gripping the side of his bloodied shirt. "Someone has already shot me once today. That's why he was driving like a maniac. We can drop you a few miles up the road -- somewhere safe. Otherwise I would start running, cause that sounds like a lot of them."

"Go to hell," Stacy said, turning away from the truck, her arms crossed as she knelt next to her man's body. Twigs crunched and leaves rustled in the distance. Faint groans of the dead escaped out from the treeline.

"We have a camp, a couple miles north of here," the old man said. He reached his arm out and Maps helped pull him up into the truck's bed. He sat down next to Garret, wiped the sweat from his forehead, and extended his hand. "The name's Anthony."

Garret shook his hand.

"I don't trust these guys," Cody said. He exchanged an intense glare with Maps.

"I'll take my chances. These men would have already killed us if they were going to do it," Anthony said.

Alyssa grabbed her backpack and walked past Cody. She climbed into the back of the pickup and turned to her brother, who gave her a disapproving glare. "I'm done walking."

Cody shook his head and opened the passenger side door after the Irishman unlocked it. Cody slung his backpack off and set it between his legs, and reaffirmed his grip on his AR-15 rifle. The Irishman's sour look didn't stop him from adjusting the seat belt.

They could see dozens of cold, empty eyes appear from the brush. A hot stink wafted across the road with their arrival. A tall man in track pants and a mud covered wife beater shirt shambled out of the woods. Dried paste like strands of flesh hung from its left cheek. The monster saw Stacy and lifted its head, taking a preemptive bite. Its teeth clacked together loudly.

"Stacy, please. Just get in," Anthony said.

Stacy cried and shook her head, trying not to turn around to the legion of corpses closing in from behind.

"We have to save her," Anthony said, standing up.

"She made her choice," Alyssa said, and pinched her nose as the hot stink of rotting flesh contaminated the air.

"Time to go," Maps said and slapped the roof of the truck twice.

The Irishman shifted the gears back to drive. He looked at the reflection of the broken woman in the rearview mirror. Her silhouette slowly disappeared behind the hill as he drove. It disturbed him. Not because he killed her boyfriend and left her behind to be torn apart. It was the complete absence of guilt.

$\approx$

The Irishman drove the truck up a gravel road, keeping his eyes on the path instead of driving like a reckless madman. Splattering another survivor across the roadway wouldn't be a good look. It surprised the brute how the small group of strangers were so quick to leave their friend behind. Perhaps they had adjusted to the new normal, he thought. Good. Most people were too weak. They struggled to make snap decisions, especially hard ones involving life or death. But to the Irishman, it was just another boring day. His humanity had disappeared long before the world ended.

The truck's wheels crunched over the gravel, a cloud of dust billowed into the air behind them. An army of trees encased the tight, winding road. The sun quickly retreated behind the horizon, casting gloomy shadows over their path. They turned into a dirt parking lot. A large sign with the text "Cloud Austin Summer Camp" carved deep into the wood rested next to a large cabin.

"Your camp is literally a summer camp," Garret said as they pulled into the dirt parking lot. He almost laughed, but figured that would only hurt. His gunshot wound pulsed furiously, sending terrible waves of pain through his system. Ignoring the immediate pain, Garret smiled at the sight of a fenced in perimeter that wrapped around several rectangular log cabins.

As soon as they parked, Cody hopped out of the truck, not giving anyone in Garret's party a second look, and walked towards the building, AR-15 swinging from his back.Alyssa said bye and jumped out of the bed of the truck to follow her brother.

"Still got close to half a tank," the Irishman said out the open back window.

Maps nodded. He finally laid his shotgun down in the truck bed and whipped out a various assortment of street guides and map books.

"Sorry again for..." Garret stopped, realizing his apology meant nothing.

"Dave always led the charge. Never could get him to stick with the group. He liked to clear ahead for us," Anthony said.

The old man let his mournful gaze tilt to the dirt. "As awful as your timing was, you saved our ass. Our piece of garbage sedan broke down on us, while we were on a supply run. There was this amazing farm, like something out of a painting, even had a white picket fence, and all the classic fixings. Found some expired junk food and cola. That made Alyssa happy, at least. But in the basement..." Anthony stopped and put a hand to his forehead as he searched for the right words.

"In the basement. There were forty or fifty of them just congregating down there, like nothing I'd ever seen. It was like they were waiting for something. Anyway, one of them saw me creeping down the steps, and all hell broke loose. Damn sedan wouldn't start.Thought we lost the mob a couple miles back."

"Those fuckers are persistent," Garret said.

Garret didn't know if what Anthony had seen was exaggerated or not, but earlier he had seen one corpse jump, and another one almost blew out his eardrums. Either way, their newfound behavior didn't sit well with him.

"Come see our doctor, she can fix that up for you," Anthony said.

"Can't, we need to get going."

"Where to?"

"Pennsylvania." Garret looked over to Maps, who continued to plot their course.

"That's quite a drive. I'm guessing there is something important there for you."

"Home," Garret replied.

"And booze," the Irishman added.

Maps lifted his head from the street guide book. "Go see the doctor. You need to get the buckshot out, clean and sterilize the wound. Or you won't be alive for Pennsylvania."

"Okay," Garret said. The stick man never spoke much. So when he did, Garret always listened.

Anthony and Maps supported Garret with ease as they pulled him through the front entrance of the main cabin, which led to the camp and fenced in perimeter.

It was all a blur for Garret as he floated through the camp. A mosaic of faces passed by him, none of which he recognized. Smoke from a barbecue pit ran through his nostrils, bringing back memories of the past summers he had spent with his family. Before he knew it, he was lying on a heavy wooden table. He swallowed a blue pill without question.

The doctor introduced herself, but her name was lost on Garret. She was just a pretty face that reminded him of his wife. His Emily. Before she even started pulling the shotgun pellets out of Garret's abdomen, he passed out.

5

DARKNESS ENGULFED THE SUMMER CAMP. Maps and the Irishman counted about twenty survivors occupying the camp. They trailed behind Anthony, who gave them a brief tour, introducing the Irishman and Maps to everybody that walked by as travelers just passing through.

Men and women hung wet towels and outfits on clothing lines to dry. Kids chased each other around the side of the bunkhouses, reclaiming moments of their stolen youth. A fire pit raged a couple yards outside of the row of cabins. A few men stood around roasting squirrels and cooking a communal stew in a massive pot. Lawn chairs surrounded the fire.

Logan, a short stick of a man, asked about Stacy and her boyfriend. Anthony solemnly shook his head and said, "They didn't make it." There was nothing more to say. Anthony didn't find a reason in placing blame on the Irishman's reckless driving or spilling extra details. Thankfully, Logan didn't press any further. They all had their fill of shitty news for a lifetime.

Logan lifted a mason jar full of clear liquid up to toast. "To Dave and Stacy," Logan drank, and the few men with jars raised them in unison.

"That moonshine?" the Irishman asked.

"Apple pie," Logan responded.

"You got another one of those?"

"This right here is liquid gold. I can't just be giving it away."

The Irishman pulled the .38 from his pocket, showcasing it in the palm of his hand. "It's got six bullets. Gotta be worth at least two jars of apple pie." The Irishman passed the gun to Logan.

Logan held the gun closer to the firelight to inspect it. He pushed the cylinder open and checked the rounds. He pushed it back in line with the barrel. Even the flames casting shadows on the Irishman's face couldn't mask his thirst.

"One jar," Logan said.

"Two jars, mate."

"Can't do it. Only two jars left and then I'll be the one drinking fucking prison wine."

Logan extended the gun to the Irishman, handle first.

"Two jars. One apple pie and the other whatever liquor you got," the Irishman said.

Logan smiled and closed his fingers over the gun and stuck it away into the pocket of his baggy sweatpants. He got up from his dirty white lawn chair and disappeared into a bunkhouse behind them.Minutes passed, which felt like an eternity to the thirsty brute.Logan returned with two jars and handed them to the Irishman, who snatched them away from Logan like the booze was a winning lottery ticket.

The Irishman twisted the cap off the apple pie jar and took a massive swig. The shine crashed through the back of his throat. He savored the searing sensation caused by the gasoline-like substance.

"Goddamn. That's good stuff," the Irishman said.

He turned to Maps and almost offered him a drink, but stopped himself, deciding it was too good to share. Maps shook his head like a disapproving father and sipped water from his canteen.

"Don't look at me like that, asshole," the Irishman said in between gulps.

Maps didn't approve of the trade. But as rare as guns were, the Irishman refused to put a price on a buzz. He twisted the lid off the other jar and sniffed it. It smelled like vomit mixed with rotten fruit, sporting a hint of alcohol. The Irishman figured it wouldn't taste too bad if he finished the apple pie moonshine first.

"Jesus, man. You're going to black out if you keep going like that," Logan said, sitting back down in his lawn chair, amused by the alcoholic.

The Irishman took another deep swig, and the jar was almost half-empty. "Don't worry about me, this ain't my first drink." He held up the second mason jar, still full of disgusting prison wine.

"Where are you from?" Logan asked.

"Grew up in New York. My father was Italian and my mother was a Jew." The Irishman took a seat in an empty green lawn chair by the fire pit. He took another sip and leaned toward the metal rod skewered through a squirrel over the flames. "That almost done?" the Irishman asked.Before Logan could respond, he had taken another sip of shine and continued talking, not caring if anyone listened to him or not. The buzz hit him hard, and that always loosened his lips.

Maps had seen and heard enough of the Irishman's bullshit for one evening. Whatever yarn he was spinning, Maps wasn't interested in it. The last time Maps had seen the bloke drink, the Irishman claimed he'd grown up in Montreal and had rambled for ninety minutes, making up the facts as he went on.

His skinny legs carried him away from the smoke and the fire. Despite the enticing smell of burnt squirrel and brown goopy soup, Maps settled for his own protein bar. He didn't know these people, and he would not eat their food. Not that he feared their intentions, rather he didn't want to be indebted, even if it was just for a single warm meal.

As Maps strolled around the perimeter, the chain-link fence failed to put his mind at ease. He had seen no guards or lookouts. Maybe these people thought they were safe, that a simple chain linked fence was enough to keep them secure, but Maps knew better.

He followed the perimeter of the fence, focusing his ears to the woods and the darkness beyond the camp. He tilted his head up to the starry sky and cringed at the sight of a gray puffy smoke trail filling the sky with a "COME KILL ME" sign.

Someone was behind him. He could feel their eyes on his neck. Maps turned around, ready to pull the knife from his sheathe and drive it into flesh. But it was only Anthony.

"Hey, didn't mean to sneak up on you like that," Anthony said.

Maps continued to trace the fence, paying no attention to the old man who followed behind him. Eventually the fence led them back to the main entrance, a small rickety cabin, its wood grayed and eroded from years of weather. The steps creaked as he made his way to the door.

"Where are you going?" Anthony asked.

Maps opened the door and entered the shack without answering Anthony's question. A front counter and two large windows gave him a view of the parking lot. Maps despised the single entry setup. If bandits or a horde of zombies wanted to, they could block off their exit with ease. Maps walked out into the parking lot, towards their newly stolen pickup. He grabbed the shotgun from the truck's bed.

"What do you need that for?" Anthony asked.

"Security." Maps turned back to the camp. Anthony followed him like a gnat on a horse's ass, grinding away the last bits of Map's patience.

"What do you mean?" Anthony asked.

Maps stopped outside of the front door to the old shack. He lowered the shotgun, pointed it to the floor, and turned to the old man. "Nobody is standing guard, half of them are drunk and even the doors are unlocked. "I'll take first watch."

Anthony stopped in his tracks as Maps walked past him like he was nothing but a speck of dust. He walked back towards the camp, his stickman shadow cast across the dusty wooden wall. Shotgun in hand, he paced the perimeter of the camp, hoping the doctor would fix Garret fast so they could forget about this place and move onward.

Garret drifted in and out of consciousness. The doctor must have been doing a good job because he was still breathing. Whatever she had given him was working some magic. The dark lines and spots in the woodgrain ceiling danced above him, warping around in circles. Who was she? Her face flickered in and out of his mind. A mixture of his wife and the doctor blended together in his head.

Unease and fear swirled around him, encasing him. Trapped without her. Afraid that he was forgetting Emily's face. Her voice echoed in his head. The sounds of her humming while she made them coffee in the morning.

A grenade full of memories exploded through his head. Years flew by in a flash. Finally, he remembered his wife's face. Her gentle eyes, soft voice and long silvery blond hair came flooding back. But with the warmth came an endless sense of sadness and mourning.

Emily hummed the same cheerful tune she always did in the morning as she fixed them a hot pot of coffee. When she'd try to wake Garret out of his slumber, her hum faded into the distance. Garret chased after it, ignoring the clinking sound of pellets being dropped into a ceramic cup.

The light blinded Garret in such a way that he thought it was Emily who tended to him now. It was just another sunny morning, and they were waking up together. But he couldn't see her face. That goddamn light was in the way. He reached out to slap the light away, desperately trying to see his wife's face, but his arms fell short. Her hand grabbed his arm, which helped settle him. Her touch was soft, but he didn't remember those callouses. She gave his hand a squeeze, and Garret smiled. Another pellet fell into the cup.

"Breathe," she said.

But it wasn't her voice. His consciousness faded again. The hanging lamp wavered back and forth from the night breeze that rushed in through the open cabin window. With the cool night air came sounds of sirens and the crack of a gunshot. Garret's instincts cried for him to move, but his body was numb, medicated, and he fell back into the dream. He hoped Emily was still waiting for him.

6

FLASHING lights painted the camp in a hellish saturation of red and blue. The whirring of police sirens snapped the campfire celebration into pieces like bones tossed in a wood chipper. Some people knocked over their chairs as they scrambled out of the center, running to grab their families and hide. A few men ran together towards the noise.

Almost every lawn chair was empty except for one. The Irishman was still kicked back in his chair like he was sunbathing on a beach, while a hurricane punched its fists through the sky towards him. The last drop of shine from the first jar hit his lip. He responded to the jar's unwillingness to generate more alcohol by tossing it into the fire. He put his hands behind his head and took a long stretch, savoring every moment of his inebriation.

Doors to the cabins slammed closed. A group of people pooled near the entrance of the camp. Among them stood Maps, Logan, and Anthony, while a few more hesitant people emerged slowly from the cabins. One man carried a baseball bat and another an axe. Logan fiddled with his new snub-nosed revolver.

The location was shit for a tactical engagement. Maps leaned against a wooden camp activity board, knowing it wasn't any better than taking cover behind a wet piece of paper. These cabins sure as hell weren't bulletproof either.

Cody joined him on the other end of the board with his AR-15. His sister Alyssa stuck to his back like a sweat drenched t-shirt. She held a 9MM Glock variant. Maps made eye contact with Cody and shook his head. Maps could see right through these people. This was their "defensive" line. They were greener than grass. The fight was over, and the bullets hadn't even flown.

Sirens of three police cruisers howled outside in front of the camp. Italicized text that read, "Greensville County Sheriff" was plastered on the side of their cars. The three vehicles rolled to a stop. Guns and spot lights pointed out from the windows at the camp. A final county Sheriff's truck pulled up behind the parked cars. The door opened and a man wearing a dusty forest green police jacket stepped out.

The Sheriff was short and fat. If the truck didn't have a step on the side, he would have had to ride in a regular cruiser. He tucked the brim of his pristine cowboy hat down, making sure it wouldn't pop off his fat, sweaty head. A clean badge rested high on his breast as he huffed out his chest and walked towards the front of the fence.

The police cruiser engines hummed him on to center stage. A few of his deputies got out of their cars to back him up with rifles and pistols aimed toward the camp. Not one deputy dared to step in front of the Sheriff's limelight. He needed everyone to know that he was the star of the show.

"Alyssa, go back inside," Cody said.

She didn't move, and it was too late for him to do anything about it.

Maps put his back to the kids next to him and leaned into the hardwood stock of his shotgun, eager to feel its recoil buck against his shoulder. The Sheriff was clean in his sights. With a quick squeeze of the trigger, he could seal his death warrant, along with everyone else's in the camp. One shot was all it would take to turn the camp into a war-zone.

Anthony walked unarmed, with both hands extended high in the air, to meet the Sheriff at the fence in front of the camp.

"Crawford, I mean, uh, Sheriff Crawford, what's this about? At least turn the damn sirens off. That's going to attract those creatures."

With a wave of Crawford's stubby hand, the loud squeals of the police sirens stopped, but the flashing lights remained.

"Anthony, harboring fugitives was illegal last time I checked, right?"

"What?"

"That nice pickup you got out here," Sheriff Crawford said, pointing to it. "Bandits stole it after they killed two of my deputies."

"We know nothing about that," Anthony said.

"Anthony, you know I'm a fair man," Crawford said. He licked his lips and leaned forward. "Don't you fucking lie to me in front of your own people." The sheriff looked past Anthony to the scared folks behind him. "Harboring fugitives from the law is illegal. I can arrest all of you. Don't have sympathy for these goddamn murderers!" Crawford shouted.

Anthony tried to reply, but before he could speak, Crawford cut him off.

"You knew Reed when he was a kid working at Albert's. Well, one of those bastards slit his throat so deep his fucking head nearly fell off when we tried to carry him off. They mutilated Sawyer, too. The man's guts fell right out of his belly," Crawford said and turned his head back to a cruiser, "Bill, show them."

Deputy Bill opened the back of his police cruiser and a dead Deputy Sawyer tripped out of the door, his hands bound behind his back with a pair of handcuffs.He crashed forward to the ground, his head thrashing in the dirt.

"Come on, bring him here," Crawford said.

Deputy Bill pulled Sawyer's corpse off the ground by his arms and pushed him against the fence. Sawyer groaned and tried to turn around, but couldn't. His lower stomach was nothing more than a cavity that used to house organs. A hard line of dried blood and shredded, loose flesh showed where the knife had sliced through him.

Anthony averted his eyes. Almost everyone in the camp had lowered their weapons besides Maps and Cody.

"Give them up. Or are you going to make me drag them out?" Sheriff Crawford asked.

"What are you going to do to them?" Anthony asked.

"Arrest them, put 'em on trial and convict the murderers. Ain't nothing changed around here Anthony, I'm still the law in this town."

Logan flashed a look at Anthony and blurted out, "One of them is right there!" Logan pointed his finger to Maps, and the deputies swung the barrels of their rifles toward their target.

Anthony turned to Logan and said, "Shut up."

"Drop your weapon, son," Crawford said.

Maps handed the shotgun to Cody and stepped out from behind the wooden post.

"Mike, is that the man that killed Reed and Sawyer?" Sheriff Crawford asked.

Mike peeked out from the back of a police cruiser and nodded. His head and broken jaw were wrapped in bandages. His lips parted in a smile, revealing his missing teeth.

"Alright, now the other two," Crawford said.

"Crawford, please," Anthony said.

Sheriff Crawford's face flushed red with anger. He looked so angry Maps wouldn't have been surprised if steam blasted out of his ears and knocked off his ugly cowboy hat.

"Anthony, maybe you couldn't hear me through this fence," Crawford said, and stepped back with an open hand. Another deputy handed him a pair of steel bolt cutters. Crawford started snapping chain links from the fence."You've always been a soft prick," he said, snapping another link of the fence with each word until there was enough room for him to step into the camp with Deputy Bill by his side. "Where are the other two? I know this guy wasn't the only perpetrator."

"There's only one more, the other one died from a gunshot."

"If you 're lying, that's obstruction and I'll take you in too. You'll hang for it."

A woman walked out of the cabin, catching Crawford's attention. "Scarlet, baby girl, it's good to see you."

She tried to hide her disgust and held out her two red stained hands. "He's not lying, Sheriff. I couldn't save him."

Sheriff Crawford grabbed her arms and pulled her closer. He held them up and examined her hands, holding them longer than necessary. He leaned in close to Scarlet, his nostrils hovering over her neck, and sucked in her scent like a wolf. Finally, he ran a hand through her auburn hair. Scarlet pulled back, hoping he couldn't hear her heartbeat thumping in her chest. The Sheriff was in some kind of mental trance, unsure whether to believe her line of bullshit.

Deputy Bill cuffed Maps and pushed him out through the fence. The Irishman stepped out of the shadows, stumbled forward, and barely caught himself on a wooden post. "Ah fuck," he said, then laughed and swayed forward, "Maps, that moonshine was something else."

Map's face turned to stone when he saw the Irishman stumbling around like a drunken fool, about to ruin a dinner party by wandering in and pissing all over the table and guests. Maps tried to catch his attention, to give him some kind of signal to keep his loud mouth shut, but the Irishman was too drunk to catch any subtle nuance.

Deputy Bill struck Maps in the face, breaking his nose, and tossed him into the back of his cruiser. "That was for Reed," Bill said and slammed the door.

"This a joke?" the Irishman asked as he stepped closer. Then he saw Mike leaning out of the cruiser's window, waving his arms wildly. "Haha, I knew I should have fucking killed you," the Irishman said as he grabbed the pair of brass knuckles from his pocket and slid them over his fist, ignoring the several guns pointed directly at him. He glided toward Mike as if he were on autopilot.

The group of deputies leaned into their rifles, ready to shoot. Crawford waved his arm, and they lowered their weapons. Before the Irishman could get within a breath's length of the open fence, Crawford unhooked a taser from his belt and fired.

Two metal prongs pierced into the Irishman's right breast. For a moment, the taser didn't seem to work. The Irishman took another two steps forward before he recognized the fiery electric current surging through his system. The Irishman slammed hard into the ground. His chin caught the brunt of the fall, leaving a patch of his skin on the gravel. Another surge of electricity coursed through him, causing him to flail about in the dirt like he was doing a pathetic version of the worm.

"Ya, done?" Crawford asked as he stepped over the Irishman and gave him a swift kick to the gut.

The Irishman, disoriented from the shock, spit blood and tilted his head back, leaving him with an upside-down picture of the audience staring at him.

"That's enough," Anthony said, as sweat rolled down his brow and into his wide eyes filled with fear.

Sheriff Crawford pulled back his boot and swung it again, but the Irishman lurched his hands out and caught Crawford's foot. He opened his mouth wide and sunk his teeth deep into Crawford's shin. The Irishman felt the enamel of his teeth scrape against bone. Crawford howled like a wolf caught in a bear trap.

Crawford's pack rushed to his aid, leaving the Irishman covered in bruises and fractures from the symphony of their batons smashing against his frame. Finally, the Irishman let go of the Sheriff's foot, but not before he vomited a disgusting mixture of blood and apple pie moonshine all over Crawford's neat boots.

"Want me to put this dog down?" Deputy Bill asked.

"Keep them separated. Throw him in the back with Sawyer," Sheriff Crawford said as he limped off stage, his show ruined by the drunken idiot.

The Irishman looked like he lost a fight with a trash compactor but still wanted a rematch. Blood streaked down his face, forming forks and rivers out of the dirt on his cheeks.

"Alright, that's enough," Crawford said as he tipped his hat to the camp and turned around for his exit. "You can have his teeth after the trial," he said to Mike, who slapped the car door twice.

The brutal beating ceased. A true fucking miracle, the Irishman thought as they put him in cuffs and dragged him to the back door of the police cruiser. He lifted his head to see the other passenger, Deputy Sawyer, in all of his dead glory. The beast snapped at the Irishman, baring its teeth. The deputies opened the door, kicked Sawyer back, and tossed the Irishman in the back with him. They slammed the door and drove off.

The Irishman struggled to keep Sawyer off him. He kicked his feet into the zombie's chest, pinning the bastard up against the car door. Waves of pain punched its way through the moonshine's effects. And it only got harder to keep the corpse off of him when the deputy took a sharp left turn. The car bounced, and the Irishman gritted his teeth as his feet lost their stranglehold on Sawyer. The corpse tried to lunge forward on top of the Irishman, but the car turned again, this time in the Irishman's favor.

In the rearview mirror, the deputy caught the exciting show. He watched as the Irishman kicked Sawyer repeatedly in the head. Not wanting the battle to be over so soon, the deputy slammed his foot on the brake.

The Irishman and Sawyer slid forward and collided on the hard plastic divider. The Irishman's head spun from a combination of the moonshine and baton strikes. He felt sick -- feverish with adrenaline. His heart slammed itself against his ribcage, faster and faster. With each beat, the Irishman kicked as if he were trying to bust through concrete. He stopped when Sawyer's skull cracked open beneath his boots.

The Irishman sat up, covered in Sawyer's blood and his own. He wondered if Maps was having a better time in the cruiser in front of them. Bruised and swollen, his head throbbed, and the hangover hadn't even kicked in yet.

7
———

GARRET WOKE up in a fleeting state of bliss before reality came crashing back over him. His heart sunk deep as if he were on an infinite drop of a never ending roller coaster. He didn't recognize the room he was in, but he recognized the dulled sense of pain in his side. Garret ran his hand across the clean bandage over his wound. Underneath it he could feel threaded stitches. Maybe these people weren't psychos. The fact that he was still alive was quite a good sign.

Garret sat up and looked at the uniform line of eight single beds extending to the front of the room. There was only one other bed occupied by an older woman with white hair. Clumps of sweaty, matted hair stuck to her face, covering one of her sunken eyes. Her body trembled, and she uttered something incoherent with each sharp breath.

As he stood up, the front door opened, and a woman stepped inside with a white linen rag and a bucket of water. The sight of her sent a wave of vague images from the previous night through Garret. As his memory slowly returned, he took a step towards her and the pain came rushing back, like someone was digging a dull butter knife into his gunshot wound.

"You should lay back down before you ruin those stitches," she said, sitting on a stool next to the old lady. She hushed the woman's incoherent mumbles and lay a cool rag on her forehead.

"Was she attacked by one of those things?" Garret asked and took another step towards the door, gauging how he could move his body without ripping the stitches open.

"No, she came down with the flu last night." She looked up at Garret. "I'm not kidding about you staying in bed. You were lucky enough to only be grazed by those pellets. I probably went overboard with giving you those painkillers last night. If you keep putting on fresh bandages and cleaning the wound, you'll be fine."

"Thanks for saving me, uh, what's your name?"

"Scarlett, but my friends call me Red."

"Have you seen my friends around?" Garret wondered if the two had ditched him in the middle of the night. He knew they despised other groups of survivors. Not that they hated humanity. At least Garret didn't think they did. They just hated the unpredictable nature of people. Both the Irishman and Maps had warned him never to trust anybody.

Scarlett lowered her eyes and turned back to the elderly, mumbling woman. "The same friends that ran over David?"

Scarlet's bluntness struck a chord in Garret. He'd nearly forgotten about the poor man that the Irishman splattered on the road yesterday."I'm sorry about that. It really was an accident."

He knew his words wouldn't provide much comfort.

"It's okay. Awful shit happens everyday now. I guess we should be used to it," Scarlett said, keeping her focus on the old woman, unable to meet Garret's eyes. "You should go talk to Anthony."

Garret found Anthony outside tying the fence back together with chicken wire and duct tape. Logan fed him the wire as he wove it through the fence. A group of five men were defending the outside of the fence like a gang of rednecks, holding baseball bats and broken table legs. Garret only recognized Cody out of the bunch. Garret walked up to Anthony with care. Anthony turned around, the color draining from his face. Just from the old man's demeanor, Garret could tell he was in for some bad news.

"Where are they?" Garret asked.

"Sheriff Crawford came and arrested the two of 'em," Anthony said, and continued to feed the wire through the fence. "We couldn't do a damn thing to help them. They wanted to come in and tear the place apart looking for you too, but we said you were dead and gone. Red stuck her neck out on the line for you, can't say I would have done the same."

"Shit!" Garret banged his hand against the fence. "Who the hell is Crawford?"

"Greensville county sheriff. He was a good man, at least he used to be."

"And now?"

"He thinks he's God."

"Are my friends still alive?" Garret grabbed Anthony by his collar and pulled him into his aura of panic.

"Get your fucking hands off him," Logan said, dropping the chicken wire and rushing to Anthony's side.

Garret let go, and Anthony fell back, trying to catch his breath. Garret braced his bandage with his hand. The pain reminded him that any exertion had its consequences.

"They'll be alive until after their trial. Without a doubt, Crawford will convict them and kill 'em quick afterwards," Anthony said and straightened himself. "And I don't know how much quicker those trials have gotten since I left."

Garret ran his hands through his hair. A nauseating lump of anxiety caught him in his throat like a barbed fish hook.

"Thanks to you douchebags, we've been cleaning up stragglers all day." Logan pointed to the pile of corpses in front of the camp.

Garret ignored Logan and asked, "So, where are they exactly?"

"Asshole I'm talking to you," Logan said, walking past Anthony and closing in on Garret.

"He has at least ten men and maybe fifty people he protects. And those people view him as the second coming of Christ," Anthony said.

"Where?" Garret asked as he shifted away from Logan.

"Asshole, listen to me when I talk." Logan pushed up in front of Garret with a puffed out chest.

Garret turned to Logan, finally acknowledging his dismal existence and

said, "I'll listen when you have something to say." Logan backed down and
spit a loogie into the dirt before shoving past him.

"You can't save them. I know they were your friends but just think, there
are people here you can help. We need more people like you and Red and
fewer people like Logan and his crew. You're smart or else you wouldn't
have made it this far. I'm not telling you where they are so you can go kill
yourself and get us killed, too. They think you are dead, we saved you, and
if Crawford finds out we lied to him..." Anthony would have continued with
his warning, but Garret walked past him. Anthony stopped talking, his jaw
half open with the rest of his words still on the cusp of his tongue.

Should he abandon them? Garret wondered. Surely they would do the
same if the situation was reversed, right? Garret would have been dead ten
times over if he hadn't run into them in that mall in Miami. Without them,
his chances of seeing his wife again were close to zero. No, this couldn't be
happening. Not after they'd come this far.

"Your friends are at the police station and courthouse back in town,"
Cody said and handed Garret the shotgun Maps had been using. "You just
got to follow the road till it splits west. Clarkson Street heads straight into
the center of town where the courthouse and police station are." Cody
checked behind him to make sure his sister wasn't around. "I'll help you if
you help me."

"Help with what?"

"I have to get my mom out of there."

"Tell me everything you know about the place. Get some paper. I need
you to draw the whole layout. Every detail you can recall is important. You
do that and I'll help you," Garret said and extended his hand. They shook
hands and Cody left to get his rifle, pen, and paper.

8

THE POLICE STATION was larger than Maps imagined. They dragged him into the basement and threw him into a holding cell. Maps sat on a cold metal bench bolted to the floor and stared at the cell wall, watching and thinking.

The basement featured several holding cells. It was bigger than what a town this size needed. He sat alone, but in the cage across from him were two teenagers. At the front of the hall, where they'd brought Maps in, was a large holding cell with over a dozen zombies reaching their tattered arms through the metal bars.

A teen cried in the cell across from Maps. His friend tried to keep him calm with a pat on the back. "John, it's going to be fine, I promise."

Maps didn't know what happened to the Irishman, but assumed he was dead or close to it. He figured that the brute's loud mouth would do himself in. These people didn't seem like the type to entertain his brand of charm. The deputy that had dragged Maps to his cell mentioned a speedy trial and how justice always prevailed. Though Maps doubted his friend would last that long.

A heavy steel door swung open at the front entrance of the jail hall. Maps recognized two of the deputies from the night before. They struggled into the hall with a handcuffed zombie, shoving it from behind. The beast thrashed about, almost causing one deputy to lose his grip on the monster.

The deputies struck it in the back with their nightsticks as they pushed it forward, past the cell full of fellow zombies. As they neared the end of the hall, they stopped in front of Map's cell. The creature's infected yellow eyes whipped to Maps. The monster threw itself against the metal bars, shredding its wrists against the metal cuffs like its skin was papier-mâché.

Maps made eye contact with the two deputies that brought him in last night.

"Feeling lonely? Well, you're going to die worse than getting torn apart by this bastard," Bill said.

"Stand back," the other deputy said to the kids in the cell across from Maps.

John stopped crying as his friend pulled him up and they both backed against the wall.

"Please don't. I'll never steal again, I promise. I'm so sorry," the kid said.

"Yeah, you will be."

The second deputy unlocked the cell while deputy Bill removed the cuffs from the zombie and kicked it into cage with the kids. The teens screamed wildly as the deputy slid and locked the door in one quick motion. He hung the keys on his belt and wiped the sweat from his face as the two kids tried to put a gap between themselves and the monster. The deputies turned around and walked back toward the front of the hall.

"Why the fuck is Crawford having us arrest these things?"

Deputy Bill turned to his partner, put a hand down on his holster and said, "Think before you open your dumb mouth, Ronnie."

John, his face still wet with tears, charged the zombie, trying to push it to the ground. But the beast towered over him, barely budging from the teen's force. Like a lion attacking an antelope in the wild, the monster pinned John to the ground and snapped its teeth into the top of the boy's chest, ripping his flesh.

Anger boiled inside of Maps, his cool as a cucumber demeanor rapidly changed as he watched the attack. Heartless bastards. These weren't real police. In a past life, he knew real men in blue that would lay their lives down for others. No, these were imposters.

John squealed like a stuck pig as he panicked. The boy pushed his thumbs into the monster's eyes until they disappeared into its fleshy sockets. He tried to push the creature's head away from his body. Darkened, rust-colored blood streamed out of the zombie's eyes, covering John's face.

His friend punched the creature in the back of the head, desperately trying to help. The monster let go for a moment, then sunk its teeth into John's clavicle bone, tearing his skin open. Blood spurted from the boy's neck as his friend pulled the heavy corpse from behind, his attempt futile.

"Let my friend go!"

He kicked the zombie in the side of its head, stunning it for a moment. With all of his strength, the teenager shoved the creature to the ground and grabbed its head. His fingers dug into the zombie's malleable scalp and slammed its skull into the concrete again and again until its head finally cracked open. A river of tears streamed down the boy's face, dripping down into the ever-growing pool of crimson gore that spread across the concrete.

John stared up at the ceiling as sweat rolled down his forehead, mixing with his pain filled tears. His hand lay on the exposed clavicle bone poking out of the mess that was his ravaged chest.

"Jake," he gurgled hopelessly. Jake turned John's head to the side, causing more blood to shoot out as he coughed. John faded fast. Jake sat over him, stroking his light blonde hair.

Maps stood silent, feeling like someone had punched him in the gut.

Jake looked up from John's limp body, his eyes void of all previous hope. They looked no different from the beady eyes of the dozen monsters in the cell up the hall.

"Smash his head before he gets back up," Maps commanded, breaking his silence.

"He's my brother, he's okay, tell me he's okay. He's going to get back up, just watch," Jake said, his eyes puffy, snot dripping from his nose.

"Smash your brother's head in, Jake. He's going to turn soon," Maps said..

"No, I can't," Jake cried.

"Do you think he'd want to become one of those things? Smash his damn head in!" Maps yelled.

Jake grabbed John's skull and turned away from it as he hit his brother's head once against the concrete floor.

"Again, harder," Maps said.

Jake looked down into his brother's lifeless brown eyes, almost bulging from his skull, and released his grip.

"I can't do it," he said.

"Look at me," Maps said.

Jake turned to Maps and looked into his eyes. He didn't know this man, but he could see the anger boiling behind his icy gaze, like a tortured pit bull thirsty to kill.

"Again," Maps said, tightening his grip around the bars of his cell.

Jake grabbed his brother's head and slammed it down on the concrete until a crack echoed over the sounds of the dead growling at the end of the hall.

9

GARRET GRABBED both backpacks of food that they had brought into camp. He did a quick scan of the contents to make sure nobody helped themselves to their goods. The supplies left a lot to be desired. There was a handful of protein bars, some granola, and a can of nuts.

Cody grabbed his AR-15 and some supplies of his own before they left. He also told his sister, Alyssa, where they were going.

If Garret had it his way, they would have already left, quick and quietly. He didn't know whether Anthony would even let them leave. Plus, he knew no one in the camp would be happy that Cody was going with him. From the camp's perspective, it'd look like a suicide mission. Maybe it was. But the map Cody drew impressed Garret, giving him enough hope for it to be a successful rescue. Garret knew shooting their way in would give them the lowest chance of survival and needed to be avoided at all costs. Shit, he thought their chance of survival was already low enough.

Cody had drawn the first and second stories of both the courthouse and police station. Apparently the second floor of the police station and courthouse were doubling as living quarters for the survivors. Garret parsed over the information again and took mental notes on the armed patrols and the location of the two generators they were using for electricity.

Garret figured there must be some major fuel source nearby to allow them to keep the generators running for the past three months. But when he asked Cody about it, he didn't have the answer or he wasn't willing to share.

Cody told him, "There are a lot of good people there that are just scared."

Garret believed him and didn't want to hurt anyone if he didn't have to. But if he had to cross a line to save his friends, he would jump across it blindfolded and deal with the moral repercussions later.

Cody met Garret behind a bunkhouse at the front of the camp with Alyssa in tow.

"She's coming with us," Cody said. He handed Garret a shotgun and a handful of shells.

"It's not a good idea," Garret said and took a step closer to them, not wanting anyone else to hear.

"I can handle myself," she said, and pointed to the pistol in the holster on her hip.

"Ever kill a person?" Garret asked and turned his gaze from her to Cody. "What about you?"

Cody looked down to his feet and shook his head. Alyssa took a step toward Garret with her hands on her hips. "I've killed plenty of those things."

"Those monsters aren't alive."

"So?" she said with a face as stubborn as a brick wall. "I'll kill a man if I have to."

"Good," Garret said and checked that his hammer was still secure on his tool belt. Though he didn't admit he never took a life before either. The mere thought of such an act made him uneasy.

"You planning on killing anyone?" Cody asked, his face hard as stone.

"Only the bad guys," Garret said. He walked to the front entrance of the camp. Cody and Alyssa followed with no more questions.

Hot rays of sun cracked through the white mix of clouds. From the high angle of the sun, Garret could tell noon had passed. They had already crossed a few miles of twisted back country roads. Billows of clouds curled through the sky, forming patterns of skinny broken hands grasping toward the sun.

The heat never let up. It pounded on the back of their necks, eager to break their will. For being a teenager, Garret thought Alyssa wasn't half bad. He expected her to want to head back to camp after an hour, but she remained focused on their mission.

Cody had said the town was ten miles out. At this rate, they would be lucky to make it by nightfall. Garret looked down at the napkin Cody had drawn on. A drop of sweat landed in the center of the first floor of the slanted courthouse. His brain raced away, running through different scenarios. Half of a plan took shape. They needed a distraction to get into the jail. From there it would be as simple as handing the Irishman or Maps a gun.

Garret planned to hit the electricity, get in fast, and get out with Maps and the Irishman. If they were still alive. Oh, and get Cody's mom to leave with them. Garret almost forgot about the promise he made. From what Cody told Garret, he wasn't sure she would go along with them quietly. That was secondary.

Doubt invaded the walls of Garret's mind. Doubt that they could pull the rescue off, doubt that his friends were alive, and doubt that any of them would even survive this. Walking two kids into an early grave. How fucking brave? He tried to burn the thoughts out of his head; he imagined the blistering sun penetrating his skull and eradicating it all.

They walked a hundred yards off the road, following the outline of their path from within the shade of the trees.

"Shit, hold on," Garret said and stopped to sit on the side of a fallen tree.

Cody turned around. "You Ok?"

"God, how old are you?" Alyssa said with a laugh. "We just started."

Cody shot her a look to keep quiet, and she responded by sticking her tongue out.

"She's kidding. We used to go on family hikes a lot. So this is just like an average Saturday for us."

Garret smiled and waved the remark off, took a sip of water, and stood back up.

"She's right, let's keep moving," Garret said. When they both turned away, Garret touched his stitches, dismissing the burning pain that radiated from his wound.

A faint sound of a siren in the distance caught their attention. They stopped in their tracks, wary to move another muscle.

"Get down," Garret said and hit the ground.

Cody and Alyssa mirrored him. They all waited as the siren's volume grew louder with each passing moment. They peered through an opening in the trees out to the road. The sound wailed closer until they could finally make out the Greensville county car easing down the road about a cool ten miles per hour.

"The fuck is he doing?" Cody asked as he lined the sights up on his AR-15, using a log as a rest for its barrel.

"Can you hit him?"

Cody leaned into his iron sight and followed the driver as he rolled down the hill, but the trigger felt heavy as an anvil. The car turned a corner behind a wall of forest.

"Sorry," Cody said as he slung the rifle back behind his shoulder.

"It's fine, just would have been nice to have a ride," Garret said.

"I don't want to kill anyone if I don't have to."

"Fair enough. To be honest, I probably couldn't have pulled the trigger either," Garret said.

A marathon's worth of dead bodies swarmed down from the top of the hill, trailing after the fading siren. Groans and howls bounced off the thick trees, spawning a hellish echo. Ghoulish faces, torn bodies, and bloody hands swayed out from the forest.

"Don't move," Cody said.

"They can already smell us." Garret pointed to the corpses on the street. They shifted their movement toward the woods.

"Stay close behind me," Cody told Alyssa.

She obeyed and pulled the pistol from her holster. "There's too many."

Garret waved his hand forward, signaling for them to follow, and dashed to the left, deeper into the woods. He jumped over a log, shoved a monster to the ground, and ran past it. A gray, curly haired man with black sunken eyes formed a wall in Garret's path. It opened its arms and mouth wide, ready to snap them shut around Garret. Garret moved too fast to stop. He tucked his elbow in and rammed the curly man hard in its chest. They both fell to the ground. He swung the hammer down, cracking its skull to bits, and Garret was up again. He shoved past another two corpses.

Together they ran. Behind them, a skinny corpse wearing long sweat-pants and a hoodie skittered on all fours like a demented cockroach. It closed the gap and leapt onto Alyssa's back, taking her to the ground. She screamed bloody murder. Cody turned around and whipped the assault rifle from his sling and leaned into it to get a shot. But his sister wrestled with the monster, failing to provide an opening.

Garret shot past Cody like a bullet, with his hammer low to the ground. He swung it underhand, uppercutting the skinny bastard off her. Before the monster could recover, Garret smashed its face in with the hammer. He pulled Alyssa up, staring into the horde of monsters chasing behind them.

"Run!"

10

THE IRISHMAN SAT in the courthouse on an ancient wooden bench outside of the courtroom. Still in handcuffs, dried blood acted as glue, matting his hair to his face. His head pounded against his skull, trying to escape, and every footstep, breath, and noise further aggravated his pain.

With his right eye swollen shut and his left eye not much better, he couldn't see much, just the deputy standing in front of him with a hand on his nightstick. He looked down at the Irishman with disgust, like a dog that just shit on the carpet.

Court was in session for someone else. Another prisoner sat next to him on the creaky bench, blubbering about how sorry he was for taking extra rations.

"They're going to fucking kills us," the man said as he wiped his face.

The deputy standing watch stepped forward and brought the baton down across the man's right kneecap, cracking it hard. The man yelled out in pain, but stopped once the deputy raised the baton again as a warning.

The Irishman looked up at his captor's greasy long hair and dirt covered face. Though his uniform was clean, he sure as shit didn't look like police. The Irishman turned away before he caught the attention of the deputy's baton. He noticed the cop lacked a sidearm. The Irishman recalled a "no firearm" sign posted on the front door of the courthouse, but he had doubted that regulation was followed.

These people have lost their fucking minds, he thought. Were they all this desperate to convince themselves that their society still functioned as normal? People who couldn't face reality pissed the Irishman off. If he got these cuffs off, he'd show them the real world.

The courtroom doors opened, followed by a man being dragged out, tears streaming down his face, his feet hanging limp, forcing the two guards to put their backs into it. Guess they didn't find him innocent. The Irishman couldn't help but chuckle at the absurdity of his situation.

A gray-haired man in a suit walked out of the courtroom and stood in front of the Irishman. He wore a light blue tie stained by mustard and chili that swayed when he spoke. "My name is William Tolstein, I'm your public defender."

The Irishman burst out laughing, and the greasy deputy stepped forward, ready to strike him, but the lawyer stood between them.

"Attorney client privilege. Please give us some space, Dalton," he said. The deputy backed off down the hall.

"What's your name?" he asked the Irishman.

The Irishman sat forward and grit his teeth. Yeah, he definitely had a few cracked ribs. "The fuck kind of circus is this? That ain't a real cop. You guys cannibals or just nut jobs?"

"We aren't crazy," he said.

"If you didn't notice -- out there..." The Irishman tilted his head toward the exit and said, "Society collapsed three months ago. Whatever help you think is coming has been eaten or skull fucked to death by bandits."

The Irishman laughed again and hugged his ribs. "But here you are putting on a charade. Amusing as it is, it will fall apart, probably as soon as you run out of detergent for those cop uniforms." The Irishman leaned his head back and stared off into the bright ceiling light.

"You're in serious trouble, there's nothing funny about it. My advice is to plead guilty to the charges and testify against your friend for a lighter sentence," William said.

"You don't get it, your people should've killed us already." The Irishman shook his head and sighed.

"You need to decide, the trial is going to start soon."

The Irishman didn't say another word. He just smiled at the thought of killing every one of them.

Court was about to be in session. Deputy Dalton ushered twelve civilians into the juror box. They all condemned the Irishman as the deputy paraded him to the defendant's bench in handcuffs. The jurors booed his entrance.

"I see this will be a fair trial," the Irishman said.

As he sat down, he recognized sheriff Crawford moonlighting as a judge in a black robe and a gavel in hand. He guessed the stenographer was dead or escaped from crazyville. He doubted Crawford knew much more about court proceedings than what he learned from watching reruns of Law and Order.

"All rise, people of the court," Crawford said.

Everyone stood except the Irishman, forcing his lawyer to pull him to his feet.

"The defendant has been charged with two counts of murder in the first degree of Deputy Reed Carlson and Sawyer Kettleman and one count of attempted murder against Mike Nelly." Crawford slammed the gavel for dramatic effect and to silence the murmurs amongst the jurors.

"Mr. Tolstein, how does your defendant plead?" Crawford asked, though he already knew the answer.

"My client pleads guilty on all three charges in good faith that your honor will consider --" The cold hard metal of handcuff links cut William off, constricting his throat.

The Irishman pulled William tight against him, leaning back, forcing the lawyer off his feet. The jury screamed, and Crawford slammed his gavel until it broke. Dalton rushed from the back of the room to save the lawyer.

William pulled at the shackles around his throat, with no success. The Irishman twisted his wrists back until a satisfying pop sounded from the man's neck. Moments later, the lawyer went limp against the Irishman's chest. The Irishman released his grip, letting the corpse fall to the ground.

"Who's next?"

Dalton struck the Irishman in the back of the leg with the baton and pinned him down against the defendant's table. With his face pressed to the cold, smooth wood, he saw a sideways view of the jury's horror and disgust. The Irishman stared through his swollen eyes into their shaking souls. They looked as if they had just seen the devil himself.

Judge Crawford stood up and bellowed over the commotion, "How does the jury find the defendant?"

The room was silent except for one juror, who said, "Guilty on all charges... Lord have mercy on his soul."

Another deputy caved the back of the lawyer's head in with the heel of his boot.

"I hereby sentence you to death by the chamber. Take this sad excuse of a human away."

The Irishman spit blood on the floor as they dragged him away. He became dead weight, forcing Dalton and the other deputy to struggle with his bulky frame. He took solace because they would all be dead soon enough, anyway. Preferably by his own hands.

11

MAPS DIDN'T MIND the constant noise of the zombies groaning, rustling, and being obnoxious down the hall from him. He focused in on their noises and used them to meditate as if their cries were waves of the ocean crashing on the beach. He had slept for only two hours on the cool concrete floor. Despite being in a dark cell, this had been one of the better sleeping arrangements since the world went nuts.

In the cell across from him, Jake sat next to his dead brother. He had cried for a bit, then he must have realized it was pointless and stopped.

Jake told Maps about his and his brother's story. How it had been his idea to steal food and supplies from a closet and jet out of town to somewhere else. One of the other survivors, a woman with short curly hair, caught them and turned them in to Crawford and his boys. The same woman that had brought them juice and bread when they first arrived at camp.

Jake begged her not to turn them in. He even tried to put back the two cans of tomato soup and the box of crackers they had taken. Even then she yelled for help. Deputy Bill showed up and hauled them away. Jake cursed the woman, and the deputy slapped him across the face, giving him a bloody lip.

Per usual Maps said little, but he listened and told Jake that he had lost friends too, like that would make the kid feel any better about smashing his own brother's head open. Nor did he try to hide the fact that they would both most likely be dead in a days' time. When Jake asked, "Are we going to get out of this?"

Maps only said, "Maybe, if you listen close."

Maps could hear a single pair of footsteps coming down the stairs. The heavy metal door swung open, and Deputy Bill stepped into the dim lighting of the holding floor. He stroke his mustache as he walked past the large cell of corpses that reached out for him. His night stick clanked across the bars, getting louder as he approached.

Finally he stopped in the front of Jake's cell -- put a hand on his belt and pulled out a key ring.

"Need to get you changed into something nice for court." Bill licked his lips as he picked the right key.

Maps sat up from the cement slab and walked to the center of his cell. "Leave the kid alone."

Deputy Bill turned around to face Maps with an evil grin. "Mind your own fucking business or I'll put you in the cell with those corpses."

Maps said nothing else. He just balled his hand into a fist, feeling his strength surge through him.

Bill turned back around, and Jake threw a handful of blood into his face and open mouth. Bill threw his hands to his face to wipe the blood off, spitting, and staggered backwards.

"Son of a bitch," Bill said.

Maps reached through the bars and pulled on Bill's right arm from behind, dragging him against the bars of his cell.

Deputy Bill tried to escape, but Maps squeezed tighter, bending the man's arm against the bar until it snapped. Bill screamed and tried reaching for the gun on his belt, but Maps twisted his broken arm, bringing him to the ground. Maps snapped another bone in his forearm and then the man's wrist in quick succession.

Without an ounce of hesitation, Maps leveraged his feet against the bars and pulled on the deputy's mangled arm until he felt it tear out of its socket.

"Fucking let go, you bastard," Deputy Bill howled.

Maps released his destroyed limb and sunk his fingers into his throat, quickly drawing blood. Bill screamed and Maps tightened his grip around the man's throat. With his fingers digging into Bill's trachea, Maps drew in a deep breath and ripped it out. Blood rushed down his chest as he gurgled for help.

With no moment to waste, Maps found the key ring and unlocked his cell.

Bill squirmed on the floor in a pool of his own blood. Maps stared into his eyes before he drove the heel of his boot into the poor bastard's head.

The boy tried to advert his eyes from the mess outside his cell, but couldn't help see the deputy's eyes bulging out of their sockets.

Maps waved a hand in front of Jake's face, breaking the trance he was in, and unlocked his cell.

"Lets go."

12

—————

GARRET, Alyssa, and Cody sat on top of a brush covered hill, catching their breath.

"We put a decent gap between us and them, but they're still on our trail," Garret said.

Cody checked the chamber on his AR-15, making sure it was ready to shoot. "Yeah, I can still hear them in the distance."

A painful gasp escaped Garret's mouth as he fingered the torn stitches on his abdomen. The sharp pain almost made him regret this whole rescue mission. Shadows of doubt cast over him. But Cody and Alyssa were eager to see their mom and convince her to leave the sheriff's cult.

Through the branches Garret saw a sliver of the courthouse roof and its wide blue tinted windows. The sun was bowing out of the sky, casting the world in a shade of orange and purple. Past the dozens of trees and lush foliage, a small light on the courthouse shone brightly.

"I don't see any patrols," Garret said, followed by a ragged breath. He dabbed the sweat from his face with a bloodied handkerchief.

"We need to get closer," Cody said and looked at the brush behind him. "They won't take long to catch up."

Garret lifted the side of his shirt, revealing a gross sight of torn stitches and fresh blood running past a failed scab.

"Here." Alyssa handed Garret a roll of duct tape. "Want me to do it?"

"Thanks, but I've got this." Garret tore a piece of tape off and slapped it on his wound. He cringed at the thought of having to rip it off later.

"Where did you get that?" Cody asked Alyssa.

"Took it from the camp supply closet."

With his eyes glaring, Cody grabbed her by the shoulder. "That wasn't yours to take."

Alyssa shrugged off the criticism and pointed to the courthouse. A police car pulled into the parking lot and a man with his jaw bandaged hopped out.

"OK, they're close enough," Garret said. He saw a skinny corpse peek out from a tree thirty yards behind them. "Let's move up."

At the bottom of the hill, there wasn't much to hide behind. The trees thinned out around the parking lot, forcing Garret to lie with his belly on the dirt behind a rock the size of a lawn chair. Shit, he didn't know if this was close enough. Alyssa and Cody lay next to him, behind the cover of a spotty bush.

Garret followed Deputy Mike with the barrel of his shotgun, even though he knew now wasn't the time to pull the trigger. At first it looked like the deputy was just inspecting the rear door to the courthouse. He walked back to the police cruiser and popped the trunk, pulling out a toolbox and an armful of 2x4s.

Garret peeked over his shoulder to see a wave of the dead making their way down the side of the hill, their eyes full of hunger.

Deputy Mike started hammering the 2x4s across the door frame, barricading it from the outside.

"What the hell is he up to?" Cody asked.

"Looks like he doesn't want anyone getting out," Garret said.

Deputy Mike wedged the last 2x4 underneath the door and hammered it into the ground. The obnoxious hammering noise caught the attention of the zombies on the hill, but Mike remained oblivious to the impending onslaught of dead.

Several minutes passed before he heard the desperate moaning noise and turned to face the hill. The color drained from his face. Panic set in, and he ran like his feet were on fire, straight to the police cruiser. He hopped in and burned rubber back onto the street, peeling away.

"Guess he doesn't intend on warning his people. This is perfect, we can take advantage of the chaos." Garret revealed himself from the rocks cover and walked into the parking lot behind the courthouse. Cody and Alyssa followed with caution.

Garret hugged the rear wall of the courthouse and peeked around to the side of the building. Across the street, he could see the police station where he imagined they must be holding his friends, if they were still alive. In the police station parking lot, he saw the truck they had stolen parked in between two county cruisers.Garret approached the edge of the building and peeked around the corner, looking for anyone standing out in the street. Thankfully, he didn't spot anyone.

Cody tapped Garret on the shoulder. "Our distraction is here."

The hill no longer resembled nature. From the courthouse, it looked like a mass of moving flesh. Garret underestimated how many were following them by over a hundred. There was no point in such a distraction if they got eaten by it.

Garret waved his comrades to follow and crouched behind a pile of trash bags and garbage cans. The trash smelled like flowers compared to the stench of rotting flesh and feces rolling down the hill to their rear. If no one heard the horde by now, they would smell them soon.

"Shit." Garret spotted two people walking down the street toward the front of the courthouse. It didn't look like they were wearing any uniforms, just regular civilian attire. A man carried a golf club over his shoulder and the woman held a baseball bat.

"We know them. Bob and..."

"Jessica." Alyssa finished her brother's sentence.

"Friends of our mom -- they'll let us in," Cody said.

"OK, I'm going around to the back of the police station to get my friends." Garret grabbed Cody's shoulder. "If you hear gunshots, just get your mom and leave." Garret extended his hand. "Thanks for getting me here."

Both Cody and Alyssa shook his hand. They rushed past Garret, headed toward the front entrance of the courthouse.

Bob and Jessica spotted the brother and sister, recognizing them immediately. Bob brought the golf club from his shoulder down to his side and stepped in front of Jessica.

"Cody, boy, what are you doing here?"

"Came to get my mom."

"You know what Crawford said, you can't come back." Bob took another step toward Cody, whose right hand was on the pistol grip of his assault rifle.

"We didn't come back to stay, just to get our mom."

"Janice is happy here, sweetie, and safe," Jessica said with a smile.

Cody took two steps toward the front doors of the courthouse, but Bob wedged himself between Cody and the two heavy doors.

"Sorry, Cody, leave or we'll have to tell Crawford. We're not letting you in."

"No, I'm sorry about this," Cody said and hit Bob in the mouth with the butt of his rifle, sending the old man to the ground. Jessica ran at Cody with the baseball bat and stopped when she saw Alyssa pointing a pistol with her index finger wrapped around the trigger.

"Drop the bat or I drop you," she said, standing in the shooting stance her brother taught her, the gun steady as a stone. "Please, Jess."

Jessica dropped the bat on the ground and sat down next to her stunned husband, trying to keep from bursting into tears.

Garret wished he could intervene to help them, but knew he couldn't waste a moment. He ran across the street and around the side of the police station, ducking when he passed the windows.

Voices echoed inside the building. None that he recognized.Behind the police station was a rear door and next to that was a flight of stairs leading to the basement. Garret brought to mind the image of the layout Cody had drawn and made his way down the steps, trying to make the least amount of noise as possible. Before he could reach the bottom steps, the back door flung open. Garret stopped dead in his tracks as he stared down the barrel of a revolver.

13

THE NAME, "THE CHAMBER" gave it a real menacing ring to what was in reality nothing but a muggy hot shed held together with rotting wood and thin tin walls. The torture shack was poorly lit by the fading sun, whose rays failed to penetrate the single murky window.

The Irishman sat on a metal chair with his hands bound behind his back by handcuffs locked through a slit in the chair. A wooden work bench holding many instruments of torture rested up against the wall underneath the window. The implications of what happens in this room would terrify any normal prisoner. Yet, the atmosphere only brought back a fond sense of nostalgia for the Irishman. As bruised and swollen as his face was, he couldn't help but form a grim smile with his busted lips.

Deputy Dalton stood in front of the table, searching for the right instrument. He passed over a nail gun and reached for a hammer. The rickety front door pushed open with some effort and Sheriff Crawford stepped inside, once again wearing his pristine uniform and spit-shined badge, proud on his breast.

"All troublemakers cry. Especially the ones with tough exteriors like yourself. Usually it's while we are dragging them here to this chamber," Crawford said.

The sheriff walked in a circle around the Irishman with his hands on his hips. He leaned forward inches away from the Irishman's ears and whispered, "You think you're a hard man? You will spill tears before you die here in this shit hole. Dalton gimme that one." Crawford pointed to the nail gun.

Dalton nodded and passed Crawford his weapon of choice. The sheriff waved the tool in front of the Irishman's face, growing frustrated by a lack of response.

"Act tough, go ahead. In the end, pain breaks all men."

The nail gun spurted forward, firing a nail into the Irishman's left breast, then another an inch to the right and another. The shock of each projectile piercing his flesh caused the Irishman to convulse back against the chair. His eyes howled with pain, but his lips never parted for more than a grunt.

"Goddamn this boy has some tolerance for pain." Crawford smiled at the challenge, then laughed. "Really, I'm impressed." He put his hand on the Irishman's shoulder. "You are making this so fun for me."

Crawford saw the pain in the Irishman's eyes and turned to Dalton. "Hand me the box cutter."

Dalton passed the Sheriff a small gray box cutter. Crawford revealed the razor with a push and pressed it to the Irishman's forehead, dragging the blade in a line through his flesh. The Irishman squirmed against the metal chair, dampened by his sweat and blood.

Crawford flashed the razor in front of the Irishman's face and pushed it close to his right eyeball. The Irishman growled and tried to tilt his head back, but Crawford grabbed him by a tuft of his hair and pulled him forward. The sheriff was ready to drag the blade across his captive's eye, but at the last moment, a knock on the door saved the Irishman.

"Hold that thought," Crawford said. He lowered the box cutter and turned around to see one of the greener men he had deputized a week ago.

"Eddie, has Christ risen again?"

"What?"

"Why the fuck are you here?" Crawford asked.

Eddie rubbed his head and looked to the ground.

"Uh, there's a situation. Mike ran off before he finished, uh, finished what you asked him to do," Eddie said and waved his hand. "Uh, I would have finished it, but there are zom -- uh, suspects, several suspects approaching from the west."

"Goddamnit. Did you at least move the rest of the supplies from the courthouse to the station?"

"There wasn't much left, but uh, yes I did it."

"You know what they say, Eddie?"

"Uh, if you want something done, uh, do it yourself?"

Crawford smacked the back of Eddie's head, knocking his hat to the ground. Eddie rubbed the spot where the sheriff's palm had landed.

"Never give a badge and a gun to a pussy." Crawford turned to Dalton. "Let's go clean this shit up, and you," Crawford glared at Eddie, "stay here and watch our friend. Cut off a few of his fingers if you like, but don't kill him and don't let him bleed to death."

"Yes, sir."

Deputy Dalton opened the door and stepped outside. Crawford took a step toward the door -- stopped and turned back around. Short as Crawford was, he looked like a fat mountain towering over the Irishman, who sulked in his chair.

"Almost forgot," Crawford said, as he jammed the box cutter into the Irishman's right eyeball and twisted the razor.

Finally, the Irishman screamed.

14

MAPS LOWERED the revolver out of Garret's face and smiled for the first time since they arrived in Greensville.

"Wasn't sure I would see you again," Garret said, and looked to the kid standing behind Maps holding a nightstick by his side. "Who's your partner?"

The kid stepped out from Map's shadow and said, "Jake."

"Nice to meet you, Jake. I'm Garret, and it looks like you two didn't need rescuing after all." Garret looked at Maps. "The Irishman, is he alive?"

Maps shrugged, "Let's ask someone."

A gunshot tore through the sky, originating from the other side of the building, followed by a dozen more, each one crackling like thunder.

"Looks like the distraction has arrived," Garret said.

Maps waved his arm for his friends to follow as he led the way back inside the jail. Jake stood at the doorway hesitating, with a sense of fear in his eyes. Garret put his hand on the boy's shoulder and said, "Jake, it will be OK, I promise. Just stay behind me, and if any shooting starts hit the ground."

Garret wasn't just trying to comfort Jake with those words, but himself as well. The few firefights he had experienced were usually over before he even pulled the trigger. A month ago, Maps still had his jet black

Remington rifle chambered in .308 with a 10x Leupold scope. As a sniper, he would eliminate any threat they encountered well before they got into range.

There was only one instance when Garret pulled the trigger with intent to kill, but missed anyway. They were camping out in an abandoned construction site on the second floor where they could really feel the cool spring air thanks to the lack of walls, when two drugged out nut jobs stumbled upon Garret's group thanks to pure shit, stupid luck. Odds of them running into anyone on the outskirts of a city ravaged by the dead were worse than a broken slots machine.

The tweakers would've never made it onto the site with Maps sniffing them out, but he had gone hunting for their dinner. Maps always hunted alone; not because he preferred it, but because the Irishman would never shut the fuck up long enough for Maps to bag a meal.

So Garret was alone, suffering from the Irishman's company. The brute rambled on about a night he spent in Brooklyn with two fiery women and a pair of handcuffs, taking a sip from his flask every time the story got interesting.

A glint of moonlight bounced off a knife as a junkie crept up the stairs. The reflection gave Garret enough time to snap his joke of a pistol, a tiny derringer, out of his pocket, and fire two shots into the darkness. Following the two shots was the click of an empty chamber and a rush of panic through Garret's body.

At first, the drunk thought Garret was unhappy with his storytelling. He realized they had company as he heard a second pair of footsteps bounding up the stairs. The Irishman struggled to stand; his balance numbed by the whiskey. He swayed to the left and gripped his brass knuckles.

The addicts split to the left and right, approaching slowly, neither one of them wanting to make the first move against the beast of a man.

"Give us your shit," the red-eyed junkie said.

The Irishman stumbled forward, toward the bastard to his left. The druggies confirmed their strategy with a quick look into each other's eyes and charged the brute in tandem.

Garret held his hammer, trying to cover the Irishman's flank, but fear gripped him. He didn't want to get stabbed, nor did he wish to strike a living soul with such a primitive weapon.

The Irishman dodged to the left, avoiding a slash that would have opened his gut. He fell backward, putting his rear to the open edge of the building. Both junkies inched forward, recklessly slashing their blades through the air, their eyes growing wider each time their attacks fell short. The Irishman leapt like a tiger onto the red-eyed bastard to his left, twisted the blade out of his hand, and sent the man tumbling over the side of the building.

"Oh fuck, man," the remaining crackhead said as he backed off. "Stop man, I'm sorry, its all good." He dropped the switchblade and put up his hands. Before the blade even hit the floor, the Irishman charged him and hoisted the skinny son of a bitch off the ground. The Irishman lifted the junkie over his head with one hand on his throat and the other on his belt.

Garret just stood silent with his mouth agape, full of terror. He watched the Irishman throw the punk off the edge of the building into a pile of rebar.

"Sayonara, asshole," the Irishman said and launched a ball of saliva over the edge after him. Garret stood speechless, disturbed by the Irishman's lack of conscience. Why couldn't he just let the man go?

"Lot of help you were, dick." The Irishman shook his head. "Make yourself useful and go see if they have anything worthwhile."

With his mind racing, Garret walked downstairs and stepped outside into the construction site. He found the one junkie convulsing on the ground. His arms, legs and spine were broken from the fall. Garret didn't know if the poor guy was lucky or not compared to his friend who was suspended in the air, rebar piercing through his torso and neck, holding him up like some sick house of horrors marionette.

Garret searched the junkie's pockets as he squirmed on the dirt, mumbling nonsense. He only found two blue pills and some dryer lint.

"Do him a favor and finish him." The Irishman stood on the edge of the building, looking down at Garret.

Garret pulled the hammer from his belt and bent over the broken man. The hammer wavered in his hand. Garret tightened his grip and raised it over his shoulder, hoping to kill the man in one swing, but the man's eyes met his, the life spiraling out of them. The hammer remained frozen in Garret's hand for what felt like a lifetime. He lowered it to his side, realizing he could never make it connect with the back of his head as long as the man was still living.

Every time Garret faced taking another human's life, that memory came rushing back.

"You, OK?" Maps asked.

Garret snapped back to reality, his shotgun wavering the same way his hammer did a month ago. "Yeah, I'm good," he said, and followed Maps into the darkness.

Muffled gunshots and screams exploded above the jail as Maps, Garret, and Jake crept through the hallway, past the cells. The holding cell full of corpses lashed out against the bars, searching for flesh.

Garret did his best to ignore their incessant wails. The monsters pushed and pulled at each other, fighting for a chance to claw at Garret and the other survivors as they passed. Maps leaned against the hard metal door at the end of the hall. He put his ear to the door before pulling a key chain out of his pocket. As he tried different keys on the lock, Garret stared at the carnage in the cell to his left.

"What the hell happened here?"

Jake rubbed the tears from his eyes and said, "They killed my brother."

"I'm sorry," Garret said, despite knowing his words did little to put the kid at ease.

The lock clicked, and Maps swung the door open. Above the staircase, the sound of gunshots, coupled with the exasperated groans of the zombies, filled the police station with a symphony of chaos. Maps lead the way up the stairs and crouched at the top, motioning Garret and Jake to stay low. He peered out with his head on a swivel.

"Clear," he whispered, and proceeded out onto the first floor.

Massive windows stretched across the front and the sides of the building. To the left of the stairway was another door that led to a second flight of stairs. Heavy wooden desks were stacked up against each other, barri-

cading the entrance and most of the windows on the east and west side of
the building. The barricade left the floor almost completely open besides a
chest-high counter in the center with a crisp American flag pinned high on
the wall behind it.

They couldn't see much through the front glass door, and they didn't
want to get any closer as the battle climaxed outside.

Adrenaline pumped through Garret. His fingers tightened around the
grip of his pump-action shotgun. With every fiber of his being, he hoped he
didn't have to fire it. Maps moved quickly, making his way behind the
counter where he could peek above it to steal a glance at the action taking
place outside.

Outside, a line of seven deputies stood shoulder to shoulder, firing into
the swarm of corpses pouring in from the hill behind the courthouse. Over
a dozen civilians covered their flanks with an assortment of melee
weapons, dealing with any stray corpses that dared to break the firing line.
Deputy Dalton took a step back to reload and a man in his 50s wearing
khaki shorts and a blue tank top took his place, striking down a straggler
with his spiked club.

Crawford stood with his back against the police station door, staring out
over the organized chaos. He held a pistol in his right hand, raising it up for
a quick headshot every few moments. Bodies piled up along the front line.
Yet, there didn't seem to be any end in sight of the zombie menace. For
every corpse they put down, another replaced it from down the hill.

"Kill them faster!" Crawford yelled, his pistol raised, dropping another
body with a precise shot to the head.

Garret squatted next to Maps. "They have to run out of ammo soon,
right?" Garret asked.

Maps shook his head and peeled out from behind the counter, heading
toward the staircase that led to the second floor.

Garret took a deep breath and murmured, "Let's not get shot." He
checked the chamber of his shotgun and turned to Jake, who was already
following Maps up the stairs. Somehow, the kid was handling the situation
better than Garret thought he would.

Before Garret followed, he aimed his barrel at the front glass door, his
finger itchy on the trigger. A mere three pounds of pressure and he could

unleash a volley of buckshot into Crawford's spine. Garret shook the idea from his head, lowered the barrel, and traced Map's steps up the stairs to the second floor. He didn't have the resolve to shoot someone in the back.

Blankets, pillows, and sleeping bags covered most of the open second floor. Two corner offices were tucked away to the west side of the building, offering a perfect view of the carnage below. A few rooms were sandwiched between the two offices, a break room, and two closets. One labeled evidence, and the other an armory.

Garret took immediate notice of what looked to be a reloading press in the break room, with a bucket of shells sitting on the table in front of an empty vending machine.

Maps stood in front of the armory door, trying to unlock it one key at a time with no luck. Without wasting a moment to curse, he began trying them on the supply room door. The second to last key clicked and Maps swung the door open. The room sported rows of barren shelves. In one corner lay a five-pound bag of russet potatoes, and above it a random assortment of canned goods and a rolled up bag of chips.

Garret slid his backpack off his shoulder and tossed it to Maps, who swiped all the cans on the shelf into the pack. He looked back to see Jake, whose mouth was watering with his eyes on the bag of chips like it was an expensive steak dinner. Maps tossed him the bag of chips, zipped the backpack, and threw it on his back. Jake devoured the bag of chips and turned it inside-out, leaving no crumbs behind.

A gunshot cracked directly above them, followed by a second.

"They're on the roof?" Garret asked.

Maps nodded.

Garret saw a rare, gleeful look in Map's eyes. He was about to get a new rifle.

15

CODY AND ALLYSSA were at the bottom of the stairwell in the courthouse when all hell broke loose outside. Cody thought it would have been harder to sneak across the lobby to the stairs, but the usual guard was dealing with the onslaught of zombies outside.Atop the stairwell, a door on the second floor opened, and two men charged past Cody and Alyssa like they weren't even there. A third man trailed behind and stopped when he saw Cody.

"Boy, there's some trouble outside we could use you out there," he said.

Cody nodded, and the man continued down the stairs past him. Cody waited to make sure the man didn't recognize him and come running back up the stairs. A few moments passed, and it looked like their luck was still intact.

He opened the door and stepped into the waiting room. Nothing much had changed since the last time he had seen it. He still remembered paying for his first speeding ticket here.

When the dead came back and started eating people, turning the living into monsters -- this is where Cody, Alyssa and their mom sought refuge. The day madness struck, the local T.V. news crew urged everyone to evacuate to the community center, so they did, as did almost everyone in town that had seen the broadcast. Many people died that night.

Cody watched his best friend Derrick get his throat ripped out by his own father. Alyssa and their mom would have been dead too, if Crawford didn't show up to clean up the mess and escort everyone to Plan B, a plan Crawford made up as he went. The community center down the road turned into a bloodbath. Without a doubt, more people would have perished if Crawford didn't show up.

Since that night, everyone saw him as a savior, like he was a fat mustached Jesus Christ with a bad taste in sunglasses. Cody trusted the man till a month in when supplies dwindled and anyone who shared an ounce of criticism was arrested and put on trial. Most good men left after that. Real deputies that had served their community for years took their families and left town when they saw the writing on the wall. After that, Crawford started deputizing crooks and backwater thugs to replace those officers. So Cody took his sister and ran.

"Think mom will actually come with us this time?" Alyssa asked.

"She has to, Alyssa.We aren't giving her a choice."

Cody walked through the waiting area to a connecting hallway leading them past the private offices that were now used as sleeping quarters. Alyssa put a hand on her brother's shoulder, stopping him in his tracks.

"You going to point a gun at her?"

"No, but I'll carry her out of here if I have to."

They reached the meeting room at the end of the hall, the door already open. Several people lined up at the window, looking down at the battle outside the building. Most of them were women and children standing on top of chairs for a better look. A short woman with curly blonde hair held a rosary in her hand, saying prayers on the cusp of her breath.

"Hey, mom," Alyssa said.

The woman turned around, hard lines of stress etched into her face.

"Baby girl, I prayed for you every night," she said and ran over to Alyssa, taking the girl into her arms. She looked past Alyssa to her son standing still in the doorway with his hands gripped tight on the AR-15 in front of him.

"Cody," she said and walked toward her son with open arms. Cody embraced her, trying to fight back tears. A month ago, he thought he would never see her again.

"I'm so happy you've come back. I'll talk to Crawford. He will let you both in, I promise."

Cody pulled out of the hug. "We aren't staying here, we came back for you."

Cody could see the hope in her eyes shatter into pieces.She slapped him hard across the face.

"If your father was alive, he would take the belt to you!" His mother wound her hand back for another strike.

Cody caught her wrist this time. "Dad would have gone with us, his family. Have you lost it? Do you want to die here, mom?"

She slapped him hard with her free hand, busting his lip open. Cody let her hand go and stepped back to nurse his lip. The people that had been watching the fight beneath them now had their eyes on Cody.

"Janice, they're exiled." Lauren grasped her shoulder and squeezed, trying to offer some comfort.

Cody knew Lauren as a child. She was his third-grade teacher and used to have a bright smile with eyes that could light a fire under any third graders ass. She had also been his first crush. But now all that fire was gone. Extinguished like a cold, wet blanket thrown on a dying ember. Her soul-less eyes sent a shiver down his spine. All the faces watching him and Alyssa were foreign shells of those he once knew.

"This was a mistake," Cody said. "Alyssa, we need to go."

Alyssa shook her head. "Not without mom," she grabbed her mom's hands and looked into her eyes, tears streaming down her face. "Please mom, come with us."

Janice pulled close and hugged her daughter once more. "I can't," she said. "You've always been stronger than me ever since you were born. I love you both."

Cody grabbed his sister by the arm. "We need to get the fuck out of here."

Alyssa wiped the tears from her eyes and followed her brother out of the meeting room. A boy watching the battle below turned around, his face rosy red and smiling. He jumped up and down. "They did it, they did it! Mister Crawford did it. They won!"

16

GARRET CARRIED a shotgun and a shiny new M40A1 Remington rifle with a gorgeous 10x Leupold scope. Jake had offered to help carry a gun, but Garret declined. Maps pressed the revolver into the back of the deputy's head. "Walk slowly."

The deputy led the way down the stairs from the rooftop, back to the second floor of the police station. Outside of the metal armory door, Maps holstered the revolver in his waistband and shoved the deputy against the door.

"Open sesame," Garret said.

"Can't, I don't have the key."

Maps twisted the man's arm behind his back until the deputy's teeth scraped together and his elbow joint was on the verge of snapping.

"Jake, go wait in there." Maps pointed to Sheriff Crawford's office.

Jake obeyed the order, with a bit of hesitation at first, fearful that Maps or Garret might forget about him.

"What's your name, deputy?" Garret asked.

"Howard," he said through clenched teeth.

"My name is Garret.I don't like hurting people Howard, but my friend who's got a mean vice grip on your arm, he won't lose sleep over it.He used to be black ops.At least that's the conclusion I've drawn over the course of the three months on the road with the man."

Howard twisted against Maps, only to have his face slammed against the metal door."Fuck both of you!Crawford will squash..."The man's insults stopped as his arm snapped.

He squealed like a pig caught in a bear trap. Maps kept Howard's head shoved against the metal door as the rest of his body thrashed in pain. Maps snatched the wrist of his broken arm and leveraged it at a ninety-degree angle. Garret cringed, not wanting this torture to go on any longer.

"Howard, please," Garret said as he pulled a chair from the corner of the room and sat down next to Howard. "I'm going to ask you a few questions. I want you to respond with brief, truthful answers. Do you understand?"

"Crawford will kill me."

"Howard, I don't want that to happen."

"Fuck, Garret, please," Howard begged. Maps put pressure on the man's broken wrist.

"Maps ease up, give him some space," Garret said.

Maps released Howard's wrist and grabbed a handful of his hair instead. "I'll smash your fucking head against this door till it opens," Maps said, pulling the man's head back until he felt the hair follicles tear from Howard's scalp.

"Key's in the sheriff's desk," Howard said, gasping for breath.

Maps smashed his face into the metal door, crushing his nose. "Where is my friend?"

"Stop!" Garret said.

Howard cried out, his eyes full of panic, "Chamber, he's in the Chamber."

"Where?" Maps pulled the man's blood soaked face back from the door that was now painted with a crimson mucous.

"The woods. Behind the police station."

Maps threw Howard to the ground at Garret's feet like he was a piece of crumpled up trash. Garret looked down at the broken deputy curled in a ball, nursing his broken arm. Nausea spiraled through Garret as Maps tossed him a pair of handcuffs. By the time Garret cuffed Howard, Maps had gone and returned with a pair of keys.

Maps swung the bloodied armory door open and stepped inside. The armory was more of a closet, with rifle racks and a few shelves with boxes of ammo. Together, Garret and Maps swept the room of every bullet. When they finished, the backpack weighed over sixty pounds, leaving Garret to wonder how Maps could even carry it along with the M40 sniper rifle slung over his shoulder. Garret was already feeling weighed down by the two shotguns and the three Glocks, two of them rested in a rugged leather shoulder holster and the other in his waistband.

As they organized their newfound supplies, they noticed an eerie silence. The monsoon of gunshots outside had ceased. They stepped over Howard toward the window, looking out over the battlefield.

Crawford stood outside on a pile of corpses. Seven deputies surrounded him, showering him with congratulations and praise. Only a few stragglers remained standing. A group of fifteen citizens stood amongst the officers, their gore splattered weapons still in hand, all of them covered in sweat and loose pieces of flesh and blood.

"Today we stood together through a trial brought on by God himself. However, we stand alive and stronger than ever. I can feel his power in me. God lives. His words surge through me like electricity." Crawford raised his hands to the sky.

"Despite this trial, the Almighty has forced me to make a tough decision, for the survival of our community, for the survival of humanity and all of God's beings." Crawford stepped off of the pile of corpses, walking past his line of deputies toward his audience."But not all of us are his chosen ones. Those of you that have wives and children go to them now."

Over half of the group of civilians left for the courthouse, leaving seven men between the ages of twenty and thirty standing before Crawford in a line.

"You are God's warriors. His hand has chosen you to protect his kingdom."

Maps grabbed Garret's shoulder, motioning for them to leave. Even Garret found himself nearly as entranced by the sheriff's presentation as the rest of his sheep.

"Is he dead?" Jake asked as he stood over an unconscious Howard.

"He's just asleep," Garret said, though he was unsure of Howard's actual condition. He hoped he was okay, but the man looked beyond help.

Maps, Jake, and Garret quickly headed out the same way they came in through the basement.

Crawford stood in front of his newly deputized officers. "God has asked me to make a sacrifice. A necessary sacrifice for you to live, for me to live, for all of us to live." Crawford looked at Dalton and nodded. "Our supplies dwindle, but God will bless us with good fortune. We will find more food. But, right now we can't afford to feed those that are not God's warriors."

With the help of another deputy, Dalton began nailing wood 2x4s into the front courthouse door. Behind Crawford, one of his officers held a milk crate full of bottles and jugs filled with gasoline.

17

THE IRISHMAN ROTATED his wrists in the handcuffs, wondering if he could slip out of them if he dislocated his wrist. The deputy Crawford left to guard him looked more like a kid. An inexperienced brat. He kept playing with his hair, shifting his cowlick from one side to the other, trying not to look at his captive.

Blood streamed down the Irishman's face from what they left of his eye, coloring his grizzled, short beard. Maybe it was too much for this kid to look at, or maybe the Irishman scared him. The Irishman jolted forward in the bolted metal chair as far as the handcuffs would allow him; the kid jumped back.

"Let me go, kid. You don't fit in with the likes of them. I smell your fear," the Irishman lied. The only thing he could smell was the old shit smeared on the chair from the people who sat there before him. He wondered if they shit before or after they died.

"Not a chance," the kid said.

"Crawford told you to cut off some of my digits."

"He said I could, if I wanted."

"Sounds like a test to me, kid. Wonder what the big boss man would think when he comes back and I'm more energetic than when he left." The

Irishman laughed. "Maybe you'll sit in this chair next, I'll try not to shit for you."

"Shut up." The kid took a step closer to the Irishman. "You don't know nothing."

"I know men like Crawford. The kind who prance around like the big bad wolf, fueled by power and the fear of weaker men, but behind those shitty sunglasses he's just like us, and dies just as easy."

"I said shut up." The kid took another step closer to the Irishman, his hands shaky as he pushed the hair out of his eyes. "The sheriff is a man of God."

"I must've missed the part in the New Testament where Jesus tortured men till they shit themselves."

"Shut up. I won't say it again!"

Despite the tremendous amount of pain the Irishman felt surging through his body, he forced his best shit-eating grin. Take the fucking bait, kid. Come on, boy.

"Pussy," the Irishman said.

The kid stormed back and forth. Not liking the way the Irishman looked at him, like he was a toddler taking his first steps. No, he wouldn't take that. He wasn't a kid anymore. He was eighteen, a man. More than a deputy, he was a warrior in this new world.

The Irishman turned his face to stone in anticipation of the boy's strike. The kid hit him with a right hook, doing more damage to his hand than the Irishman's face. Blood dripped down the Irishman's swollen lip. Good, he thought. A new line of red appeared on the Irishman's cheek where the kid's fingernail had scratched him.

"That the best you can do?"

This time the kid took his time, winding up a strike, getting too close. The Irishman shot up from the chair and sank his teeth into the boy's cheek. He pulled back, tearing flesh, leaving the boy's cheekbone exposed. The wannabe deputy tumbled backwards, both hands covering his mangled face. The Irishman spit the flesh to the ground. Blood streaked down his chin. A familiar, salty taste washed across his taste buds.

Tears edged out of the kid's eyes. The Irishman hoped the kid wasn't so shocked that he would run for help. He was surprised the boy remained on the ground for this long, moaning in pure agony. Come on, get up, little bastard.

"Take your time, I guess. But you're infected just like me."

The kid looked up from the ground, hurt and confused.

"I got bit before they brought me in, check my shoulder," the Irishman said, knowing the boy wouldn't dare get that close to him again. "You need my help to cauterize it and stop the infection before it spreads through your blood and it's too late."

The kid jerked on the ground, his sheriff's department jacket ruined with red. His eyes became wide saucers of panic.

"What does the sheriff do to people that are infected?" the Irishman asked. "It can't be anything good. Get those bolt cutters and cut me out of here. I can help you."

The kid struggled to stand, his right hand glued over the hole in his face. He looked to the bolt cutters and then to the Irishman.

"Stop wasting time or you're fucked."

Full-blown hysteria spread through the young man. The boy bolted out of the shed, not bothering to close the door on his exit.

"Shit," the Irishman said, stuck in the bolted metal chair. He didn't want to die here, but knew his last chance to save himself just ran out the door. Overplayed my hand, he thought. A gambler too used to winning. It could be worse. Why fucking lie to himself? It couldn't get much worse than this. Shit, Crawford was just warming up.

A gunshot thundered outside the shed. Suddenly Garret appeared in the doorway, his face stricken with disgust. "Holy shit, you got uglier." Garret's joke fell flatter than usual.

"You took your fucking time! Bolt cutters on the table."

Garret snapped the cuffs off the Irishman's bruised wrists. Pain shot through the Irishman's stomach, reminding the brute of his broken ribs. Maps stood in the doorway of the shed, with Jake behind him.

A smile spread like wildfire across the Irishman's face. As he walked to the door, his stance wavered, and Garret caught him by the shoulder. The Irishman pushed Garret away. "I'm fine. I don't need your help."

Noting the Irishman's poor condition, Garret shook his head. "Change of plans. I'll go get Cody and Alyssa. The sheriff and his thugs must've heard that gunshot. I imagine they will investigate and scour this place from top to bottom when they see you're missing. You guys head north into the woods and I'll meet you there in fifteen."

"No," the Irishman said, and grabbed a shotgun from Maps. He walked to the workbench and aggressively ran a saw over the barrel. "I'm going to kill them all."

"We got five shooters if Cody and his sister aren't dead," the Irishman said, as he finished sawing the barrel down to the pump.

"Six," Jake piped up from outside the shed. "My dad taught me how to shoot."

Maps gave him a Glock 22, a small gun that looked large in the fourteen-year-old's hands.

"They can't have much ammo left after killing that horde. Plus, we raided their stash," Garret said.

Together, they walked outside the shed. Tentacles of black smoke curled through the sky.

"You guys set something on fire?" the Irishman asked.

18

CODY STARED out the second-floor window of the courthouse, watching as a Molotov cocktail crashed below. Fire spread across the ledge and up the wooden window frame. He stepped back, both him and Alyssa confused about what just happened. Screams echoed down the hall, and it clicked. They were burning the fucking courthouse to the ground.

"Follow me close, shoot anyone that tries to shoot us."

Cody ran out into the hall across to another office. The doorknob seared his hand, forcing him to fall back. Bodies brushed past him as he stared at the hot door, listening to the crackle of wood splitting against the flames. A slender hand gripped his shoulder.

"Mom," Alyssa said.

"God's fire."

"They're burning it down, just like the community center," Cody said.

Above them, a fire alarm hung by a thread. Someone had taken an axe to it. Cody dashed to the stairwell at the end of the hall, his sister and mother following him. The screams of men and women burning beneath him stopped him in his tracks. The roof. They had to get to the roof.

Cody led the way up the stairwell, grabbed the door handle, and tried to turn it without success. It sounded as if the supports of the second floor were giving away, collapsing onto the first floor. The impact shook the foundation of the building. Smoke filled the top of the stairwell. Cody furiously kicked the door.

Footsteps pounded up the stairs. Cody whipped around with the AR-15. A man, his face blanketed in ash, cried, "Please help me -- my son, he's stuck under debris."

Cody turned back to the door and raised the assault rifle. The man grabbed Cody by the shoulder and turned him around. "What the fuck is wrong with you?"

"Sorry, there's no time." Cody shoved the man off him and the man retreated to the bottom of the stairs beneath the rising smoke.

Alyssa aimed the pistol at the handle and shot off two rounds. With one last kick, the door opened. Together they ran out to the roof, but stopped when they saw the center of the floor sinking.

"Hug the side with me. This fucker's going to collapse," Cody said and slung his AR-15 across his shoulder.

A man appeared in the stairwell doorway, holding his injured right arm.

"Malcom," Cody said, recognizing the older gentleman. He was glad he had survived all this time, though his wife was nowhere to be seen. Cody waved the man over and leaned over the edge.

"Your plan is jumping to our deaths?" Alyssa gasped in disbelief.

"Look." Cody pointed over the edge of the building. Below the ledge were two trash cans stuffed to the brim with trash bags.

"Are you serious?"

Cody didn't reply, just slung the assault rifle off his shoulder and dropped it into the trash. He threw his legs over the side and pushed off the ledge. The terrible smelling black plastic trash bags broke the brunt of his fall. Without a moment to spare, he moved to the side, ignoring his freshly sprained ankle and bruised ass.

The center of the roof crashed down onto the second floor, shaking the entire building like an earthquake. As Cody gathered his assault rifle and limped out of the way, his sister followed him. Thankfully, Alyssa landed gracefully in the middle of the trash. Horror flooded her face as sticky trash juice splashed across her body.

Above them, Malcolm argued with their mother. "Jump."

"No, I can't."

Flames swept up the side of the building, threatening their window of escape.

"Mom, there's no time!" Cody called up to her.

Malcolm grabbed Janice by the arm and jumped with her. The edge of the trashcan clipped Malcom's injured arm. But Janice seemed unscathed.

"Thanks, Malcom." Cody lent him a hand, pulling him out of the garbage.

Ash and smoke left their faces covered in soot. Cody coughed, smoke stinging his lungs. Sirens whirred on the other side of the building. Total chaos. He clutched his assault rifle, peeking around the corner. Piles of corpses littered the street in front of the courthouse. There must have been over a hundred dead on the ground.

"Why burn us?" Malcom asked himself as he examined the second-degree burns on his hands. Burns he received as he had tried to pull a flaming wood support beam from his wife, even though the impact had certainly killed her.

Cody leaned against the hot brick wall. Flames crackled on the other side. On the street he saw two deputies, younger men. One of them he went to school with, Jay. The other was a man in his thirties, someone that must have joined up after Cody had escaped with his sister. They were talking to each other as they watched the building burn. Cody couldn't make out what they were saying. Jay let out a short laugh that twisted Cody's intestines in knots. Rage grew in the pit of his stomach. Bastards.

He raised the AR-15 and looked down at the sights. First, he watched Jay through one eye; the sights lined up on his childhood friend's chest. He inched his finger to the trigger and paused. Crawford stood in his office on the second floor of the police station, staring out to the street below him. Cody saw him and pulled back behind the wall. His heart drummed in his chest, reverberating through every bone in his body. Sweat rolled down his face. It pitter pattered down his nose like a rusty faucet. The AR-15 became heavier with each passing moment. He slid down against the brick wall and tried to catch his breath as he decided on their next move.

19

BROKEN RIBS and multiple lacerations on various parts of his body didn't stop the Irishman from leading the charge. He firmly gripped the wood grain pump of his improvised sawed-off shotgun. The Irishman preferred a short barrel. It produced a wider spread that way. It was easier to kill two or three people with one shell, though in a long-range battle, he'd rather throw it at them.

Garret walked next to him, no longer behind him in the shade of his shadow. He wondered if revenge fueled the Irishman, or if he was just eager to see if he could still shoot straight with one eye.

Poor Jake looked like he was going to vomit when he saw the brute's condition. Did the Irishman even feel pain? Garret wondered. The two of them crept toward the back steps to the basement of the police station. The door to the jail brought back a creeping sense of déjà vu.

"Maps said to wait five, till he and the kid are in position."

The Irishman hawked a ball of spit to the ground. "We ain't leaving any for them."

He recklessly kicked the door open, ruining their element of surprise. A young man in a bloodied white polo was dragging a corpse down the hallway; it was the deputy Maps had smashed into the bars less than an hour ago.

"Freeze." Garret brought the man's chest into his sights.

The man dropped the body and looked up, shocked and full of fear. Slowly, he raised his hands above his head. The shotgun blast turned the man to an unrecognizable mess on the floor. His headless torso fell backwards to the concrete. The ringing in Garret's ears made it hard for him to make out whatever command the Irishman was barking at him.

"Fuck, a warning would've been nice," Garret said, straining to hear.

"Open the door on their footsteps." The Irishman repeated to Garret. "I'm blind. Are you fucking deaf?" the Irishman slapped Garret on the back.

Garret ran to the door at the front of the jail, jumping past the two dead bodies like track hurdles. He dodged the bony dead hands, reaching out of the cell to his left. He stood with his ear to the door, worried that he wouldn't be able to hear any footsteps over the buzzing in his ears. The Irishman racked the pump on his shotgun, ejecting a spent shell in the air. It arced down into the growing pool of blood on the concrete.

Two pairs of footsteps bounded down the stairs on the other side of the door. Garret counted in his head and signaled to the Irishman, who crouched down a few yards from the door. When the footsteps reached the bottom, Garret swung the door open, and the Irishman followed up with a blast of the shotgun.

Two deputies fell on top of each other at the bottom of the stairs, their legs torn to shreds, their mouths agape in pain and terror as the Irishman pumped the shotgun and let off another slug, turning the upper half of their bodies into a paste. Bone fragments crunched beneath Garret's feet as he looked up the stairs for any other threats. The Irishman brushed past him, storming up the stairs.

"Take it easy," Garret said.

"Yeah, when they're all fucking dead, I'll think about it." The Irishman disappeared up to the first floor of the police station, leaving Garret behind.

Garret leaned against the wall with his heart bursting in his chest. Heavy automatic weapons fire exploded above him, followed by two blasts from the shotgun and then silence. The Irishman peeked out from behind the door at the top of the stairs. "You coming or what?"

Anxiety rushed through him. Is this where it all ends?

"Hurry."

Without a moment to smother his anxiety, Garret pushed forward. Two corpses lay across the first floor. Garret attempted to ignore the graphic scene. Did they all really have to die? A bullet flew by Garret's head, putting a hole in the wall behind him. The Irishman grabbed Garret by his shirt and threw him to the ground behind the counter.

Gripped by panic and fear, Garret put his back to the counter. The Irishman was lying on the ground with his face pointed up to the ceiling. "Keep low, that wood won't stop a bullet from popping your head."

Garret slid lower against the counter as a burst of fire tore through their cover. Splintered wood rained down upon them.

"Three shooters," the Irishman said.

The brute rolled out from behind the counter. The shotgun kicked against his shoulder, expelling death to whoever made the mistake of getting in the way of his barrel. He pumped it again, pulled the trigger. It clicked, empty. The Irishman rolled back into the remaining cover. A door opened, followed by the sounds of feet rushing across the tile floor.

"Shells, now." The Irishman extended his hand. Garret searched his right pocket and tossed the Irishman three shotgun shells. The Irishman loaded the shotgun faster than a machine.

"Cover the right flank, they're inside now."

A flash of light bounced off of a badge through the holes in the counter. Garret pressed the barrel of his pistol into the hole and pulled the trigger. The gun bucked in his hand as he fired two more times. The Irishman stood up and splattered the remaining deputy against the wall.

Four bodies lay amongst broken glass and scraps of wood. The man Garret shot was splayed out on the ground, looking for the handgun he dropped at his side. With his other hand, he held the gaping hole in his stomach.

"Nice shot, right in the gut. Poor fucker will bleed out in a few," the Irishman said as he stepped on the deputy's wrist, crushing it beneath his boot.

Garret stared down at the dying man with a sense of regret. Suddenly, he realized how hot it was in the building. Sweat drenched his back and his stomach did somersaults. Is this how the Irishman felt every time he killed someone? Bile crept up his throat, making Garret think he was about to puke.

"Go ahead, finish him," the Irishman said.

But the gun wavered in his hands. The deputy stared down the barrel, begging for mercy with his eyes. No, this wasn't right. The poor son of a bitch was just as scared as Garret. Unable to pull the trigger, Garret lowered the pistol.

"Good thinking, no need to waste any ammo." The Irishman smashed the deputy's skull to bits with the butt of his shotgun.

At least eight were dead, but there was no telling how many remained. It wasn't supposed to be happening this way.

The Irishman slapped Garret on the back with a bloody grin on his face. "Let's find the chubby fuck."

Garret's ears were still ringing from the shootout as they made their way up the stairwell to the second floor. The Irishman put a finger to his lips, shushing Garret.

"Step slow," he whispered.

At the top of the stairs, the door to the second floor was wide open. The Irishman motioned for Garret to stop. They waited. For Garret, it felt like an eternity.

"You hear that?"

Garret focused past the dull ringing. The sound was ever so subtle. Heavy breathing. Directly on the other side of the wall. The Irishman grinned and licked his chapped lips. He ducked down with the shotgun aimed at the bottom of the wall. Garret held his pistol out, aimed at the open doorway with a steady hand. Crawford was the one man he wouldn't mind killing.

The Irishman shot through the drywall. Four shots exploded out of the wall followed by a pain drenched scream. Garret rushed through the doorway. Crawford lay on his back with a gaping hole in his ankle and an empty revolver in hand.

"Drop it."

Crawford let go of the revolver. It clanked on the floor. The Irishman walked through the open doorway, his shotgun sweeping the rest of the floor.

"God will protect me," Crawford said. He opened his mouth for a prayer, and the Irishman shoved the barrel of his shotgun in.

Garret couldn't make out whatever muffled curse Crawford was trying to spew. Silenced by the gun, he attempted to make the sign of the cross. The Irishman stopped him, pinning the sheriff's wrist to the ground with his boot.

"Don't kill him." Garret grabbed the Irishman's shoulder.

The Irishman pulled the trigger, click. He laughed when Crawford's head didn't explode into a million little pieces. "Ah look at that, he pissed himself."

With the Irishman's help, Garret grabbed the sheriff off the ground, shoved him against the wall, and cuffed him. The Irishman pushed him forward, and together they pulled him down the stairs. Blood trailed behind them, leaking from what was left of Crawford's ankle.

Maps greeted them with a frown at the entrance to the police station. Clearly, the thin man was less than pleased with the Irishman's disregard for their plan.

Cody, Alyssa, Janice, and Malcom walked from around the side of the building.

"Jesus, you guys made it," Cody said.

"So did you. I saw the smoke, and I thought you were done for," Garret said.

Without Garret to lean on, Crawford fell to the ground.

"Whoops," the Irishman said as he scooped the man off the ground by his arms.

Maps jingled a set of car keys and pointed to the same truck they had stolen earlier. Next to it sat a single police cruiser.

Garret grabbed Crawford by the collar. "Where are the rest of them?"

He smiled with a chipped tooth, "I sent a few of em on a supply run."

"Where?" Garret slapped him across the face.

"Stop it." Cody's mom stepped out from behind her son. "Don't you touch him again." Before she could get any closer, Cody pulled her back to his side.

"He tried to fucking burn us alive!"

"That's a lie," Crawford said.

Cody raised his assault rifle at him, but Garret pushed the barrel toward the ground.

"We need him alive for now."

Malcolm walked past Garret and spat in Crawford's face, "My wife trusted you, I trusted you."

The Irishman was getting a kick out of the sheriff's fall from grace, but pulled him back from the pack of wolves. "Garret says we need him alive. So I'll take the liberty to cauterize his wound. Wouldn't want ya bleeding out on us, now would we?" The Irishman dragged Crawford against his will, writhing and cursing, toward the burning courthouse. He pushed him up the steps to a pile of embers.

"Someone fucking give this blind man a hand," the Irishman shouted.

Maps helped the Irishman drag Crawford and shove his bloody stump into the hot embers. Crawford's howls filled the sky. Anyone for a few miles could probably hear the echo. Crawford went limp, and they pulled his leg out of the fire.

Cody's mother wept for the sheriff.

"Wake him up," Garret said.

Maps slapped him across the face till his cheeks and nose were bloody. Crawford woke up gasping for air.

"Did you send them to the camp?"

Crawford didn't say a word. Garret already knew the answer. "We need to go, now."

20

GARRET RODE in the truck's bed with the Irishman and Crawford, while Cody, his family and Malcom followed behind in a police cruiser. Jake rode shotgun. Maps drove fast, but Garret felt much more at ease with him behind the wheel. The camp was about five miles away, but Garret could already hear the faint sound of gunshots in the distance.

"Fuck the camp, Garret. Let's ice this asshole and move on. We got ammo and guns."

"Those people saved me. We can't leave them blowing in the wind against those nutjobs. Scarlet can patch you up, too."

"If she's still alive," the Irishman said as he sorted through the fat bag full of ammo boxes and magazines.

"I saw two gas powered generators back there. And I noticed how much you and your deputies made use of these police cruisers," Garret said.

Crawford spat at Garret's feet. The Irishman slapped him hard on the back of his head. "Do that again, and I'm throwing you over the side. At sixty miles an hour that won't be a fun tumble."

"Where are you getting the gas?" Garret asked.

"Nowhere boy, it's all gone."

"Liar." The Irishman balled his fist and struck Crawford in the mouth.

"Sheriff, I want you to think about your reply. If you bullshit us, I'll turn my back and let that bastard sitting next to you ask the questions."

Crawford leaned forward, seething with rage. "God will protect me as I walk through the valley of darkness."

"This asshole is drinking his own Kool-Aid," the Irishman said and grabbed Crawford's throat with a cast iron grip.

"Where is the gasoline?" Garret asked, but Crawford couldn't answer. His face turned blue.

"This fat son of a bitch isn't going to tell us shit. Let me crush his windpipe, cut out his eyes and call it a day," the Irishman said.

Garret shook his head. "Let him go."

The Irishman released Crawford from his death grip. Crawford coughed, desperately sucking in air.

Gunshots thundered as Maps pulled the truck to a stop a hundred yards from the camp. He threw the vehicle into park and hopped out, taking a hunting rifle with him as he disappeared into the woods. Jake followed him.

The Irishman loaded two shells into his shotgun. "Who wants to watch this dick?" The Irishman slipped out of his shoe and pulled off a yellow stained sock. He stuffed it into Crawford's mouth.

"I'll do it," Malcolm said as he approached from the police cruiser behind them.

The Irishman hopped down out of the truck. "Cody, stay with him. I don't trust you," he said, pointing to Malcolm. "Should kill you right here for being on that bullshit jury." The Irishman swept the shotgun barrel on his hip toward Malcolm.

Malcolm stepped forward, his gut in front of the barrel. "That bastard burned my wife alive. I won't let him go anywhere."

Garret half expected the Irishman to shoot him there. Instead, he lowered the barrel and walked past Malcolm.

"Stick behind me, don't shoot me in the back," he said to Cody and Alyssa.

"Alyssa, stay with mom," Cody said. Their mom was still in the backseat of the police cruiser, her face in her hands, sobbing.

Garret, Cody, and the Irishman stuck to the foliage outside of the camp.

There were two sheriffs department cars and one truck in the parking lot. An eerie silence fell over the camp. The fight was over. Two deputies dragged a tarp behind them with one of their own laying on it, wounded.

"They are outgunned. We can get them to surrender," Garret said. "Nobody else needs to die."

The Irishman walked out of the brush and into the dirt parking lot of the camp.

"Shit." Garret backed him up with a hand on his pistol.

Garret stuck the barrel of his pistol to the back of the skinny deputy's head. "Don't move. How many are inside?" Garret disarmed the deputy, pulling the revolver from his holster. No answer.

Another gunshot sounded from inside the camp.

"Goddamnit," Garret said. He struck the deputy in the back of the head, knocking him out cold.

The Irishman took the head off his captive with a blast from the shotgun. The wounded deputy tried to roll off the bloody tarp, but his gunshot wound was too bad. He racked the shotgun again and finished him.

Cody stood outside of the brush, holding the rifle by his side. Speechless. The Irishman stood over the knocked out deputy and shot him in the back of the head.

"Fuck, what are you doing?" Cody grabbed his shoulder. The Irishman shrugged him off. "Shove that remorse back up your ass. Were you planning to nurse them back to health?"

Garret knew the remark was just as much for him as it was for Cody.

Screams blared out of the camp, followed by another round of gunfire. Together, they moved through the entrance into the camp.

Inside the camp, Crawford's remaining warriors scrambled for cover. Gunfire had torn apart the bunkhouses. Garret wondered how many dead lay inside and if they would get back up soon.

Deputy Dalton took cover behind the camp sign post with another deputy at his side. "Surrender, and we will show mercy," he yelled from behind the poor cover.

A rifle round blasted through the guts of the man next to him. Dalton slid lower against the wood. "Sniper!"

One of Crawford's men jetted from across a bunkhouse, only to eat a rifle round in the spine.

"Someone take him out, cover fire!" Dalton yelled, not realizing he was the last one alive. "Jordan, Tyler?"

"They're dead, asshole," Garret said.

Dalton threw his revolver over the side of his cover.

"I surrender, don't shoot!" Dalton raised his hands to the sky, palms open, and stepped out from the "welcome" sign.

The Irishman raised the barrel of his shotgun, but Garret pushed it down. "Enough killing."

Maps and Jake descended from a hill overlooking the camp from the west.

Dalton got on his knees and roped his hands behind his head. "Please don't kill me, please don't kill me, please don't kill me."

Garret walked into the camp. "Scarlet? Anthony?" he called out.

Garret tried to keep his eyes on the bunkhouses, off the ground, away from the corpses of women and children killed in the assault. A sickness surged through Garret as he cracked the door to the medical bunkhouse. Anthony lay slumped in the front corner of the cabin. He breathed slowly as his hand attempted to cover a gaping hole in his chest. Blood trickled down the side of his mouth.

Garret rushed to his side. "I'm sorry. Hang in there, we're going to get you patched up." Garret scanned the room for bandages. Anthony grunted. The life left his eyes as blood pooled against Garret's boots.

"No, goddamnit!" Garret slammed his hand against the wall. Two more dead lay in the bunkhouse. No sign of Scarlett.

Garret walked to the back. He found Scarlett slumped on the floor with a bullet hole where her right eye should've been. Brain matter stained the wall behind her. The sight sickened him. He stumbled back, doubled over, and spewed vomit on the ground. Did he cause this? Did he trade these innocent lives for his ruthless friends? Anthony had warned him, but Garret justified his decision. No, he didn't think it would play out this way.

Garret stormed out of the bunkhouse. Cody, Maps, Jake, and the Irishman stood in the middle of the camp. Maps cuffed Dalton and pushed him to the ground.

"He better stop whining," the Irishman said.

"I'm sorry, don't hurt me. The sheriff ordered us to do it," Dalton said.

Garret's hands trembled as he stomped past Maps and Jake.Sweat, tears, dirt, and blood covered Garret's face. He had never felt this way before. The pistol in his hand wobbled for a moment.

Something in Garret's brain clicked. The pistol became an extension of his arm. He put the barrel to the back of Dalton's head. The blast splattered the innards of his skull across the ground. Garret stood over his body as if the man were about to stand back up. The color drained from Garret's face, and he dropped the pistol to the ground.

The Irishman clapped and put a hand on Garret's shoulder. "Feels good doesn't it?"

Garret didn't respond. No, it didn't feel good. Not one bit.

21

MAPS PATCHED up the Irishman and re-bandaged Garret's wound with what remained of the medical supplies. He assigned Cody and Malcolm the duty of braining the dead. They didn't need any risers, making this day any worse.

It was a massacre. Nobody from the camp survived besides Logan and his drunkard friend Trevor. Garret found them hiding in a broom closet. They must've been sipping moonshine while everyone else was slaughtered.

"Where did that brute go off to?" Garret asked.

"The Irishman said he was taking Crawford for a walk in the woods," Cody said.

Night fell.

Outside the camp, Garret sat on the hood of the truck, a hammer at his side for any stragglers late to the party. Cody lifted himself easily onto the hood, joining Garret, the AR-15 hanging from his shoulder strap.

"He's been gone for a while with Crawford. What do you think he's doing to him?" Cody asked.

"Nothing pleasant."

"Can't believe it's all gone in one day." Cody snapped his fingers. "Like that. Everyone I grew up with, all the people in my world, dead."

Garret shifted his weight, feeling uncomfortable.

"You think it's our fault?" Cody asked.

"I don't know. I think it was inevitable, we just sped it up."

They both sat in silence, staring up at the bright stars.

"Sometimes I think about my dad. Where we would be if he were still alive. If mom would still be this way..."

"Did he die when this all started?"

"No. He died two years ago from a heart attack. I think about him now, in his coffin, scraping at the cloth lining, trying to get out."

"That's a tough image to cope with, Cody."

"Far from what I saw today. Those kids. I knew all of them. But, I don't blame you for what you did to Dalton, no one can."

Garret shook his head. "What I did was evil. I can still feel it in my gut." Garret sighed. "I need some time to myself."

"I can respect that, but one more thing."

"What's that?" Garret asked.

"I know you guys aren't planning on sticking around. I want to travel with you, with Alyssa and my Mom. We won't make it far without help. Malcolm too, he made mistakes, but he is a good man. Power in numbers, right?" Cody said.

Garret paused for a moment. "I'll talk to them about it."

"Thanks." Cody hopped down and walked back to the camp where they were starting a fire.

Hours passed before the Irishman returned alone. The day had taken its toll on Garret, and despite the excitement; he nodded off in the truck. Upon the Irishman's arrival, Maps nudged him awake.

"I'm up." Garret yawned.

He got out of the truck to stretch his legs and greet the Irishman. Maps loaded the back of the truck with two backpacks filled with food supplies and a duffel bag loaded to the brim with ammo. He tied together the extra shotguns and rifles with a bungee cord and laid them in the truck's bed.

"Let me guess. Crawford is dead," Garret said.

"Death would have been mercy," the Irishman said. "I let the fat-ass go. Don't think he will make it far with that blown off foot either." The Irishman reached into his pocket. "Brought you a trinket though."

In the darkness, Garret couldn't see what the Irishman tossed him. Something round and slick. A wet piece of an eyeball. Garret dropped it and wiped his hands off on his pants as the Irishman laughed.

"Disgusting."

"Yeah, I couldn't get the other one to pop out like that."

"You're sick," Garret said, his stomach gurgling.

"He talked after I took his right eye. There's a tanker full of gas, a couple of miles from here," the Irishman said with a smile. "Fill up tomorrow and we can put this place in the rearview."

"About that. Cody, Alyssa, their Mom, and Malcolm want to come with us."

"Too bad," the Irishman said. "We don't have food for 'em. This ain't a fucking convoy."

"Half of those supplies are theirs." Garret pointed to the truck.

"So? We're the ones with guns."

"Jake is coming with us." Maps joined the discussion.

"No shit, I know you two developed some weird father son relationship in that jail. But the brother and sister and their bat shit crazy mom is another story," the Irishman spat. "And for Malcolm, you're lucky I didn't execute him back in crazyville."

"Hey, you know what's a good idea? Let's invite Logan and his dickhead pal that hid while a bunch of women and kids got shot up. Fuck it, Garret. While we're at it, forget about your family. Let's just cruise around the country saving people."

Garret grabbed the Irishman's collar and pulled him close. "All those bodies in there are on us. None of this would have happened if we didn't come through here."

"But we did, and it's done." The Irishman broke free from his grasp and said, "After you killed that punk today I thought you grew some balls."

"That's why we can't leave them here to die. I'm not a heartless dick like you. I can't be."

"Fine." The Irishman was done arguing. He turned to Maps in passing and said, "I just want to go on record that this is a shit idea."

Maps shrugged. The Irishman kicked up dirt and walked back into camp to get some sleep. Garret lay down in the truck. The day's events replayed in his mind as he drifted off. Maps stood watch.

22

DAWN BROKE. Rays of sunlight shone through the sea of clouds. Garret stretched his neck and hopped out of the truck. He found Maps passed out in the back. It was the first time Garret had actually seen the man sleep.

Cody paced back and forth in the parking lot, eager to talk to Garret.

"Relax. I already talked to them. It's a go." Garret could see immediate relief on Cody's face.

"Thank you. Despite all the awful shit that went down, I see some sunshine at the end of this."

"We plan to gas up and hit the road. My family is in Pennsylvania. My wife Emily always thought shit would hit the fan. Maybe not like this. But anyway, it's stocked with enough food for at least six months and she insisted we install a bomb shelter."

"Sounds good. I'll go wake Mom and Alyssa. Malcolm is already up. We collected the rest of the supplies earlier. There wasn't much, a first aid kit, and some random cans of food. What about Logan and Trevor?" Cody asked.

"They're not coming."

"O.K." Cody said.

Garret made his way through the camp. They had dragged most of the bodies off to the side, but the dirt was still stained with blood. Garret saw the Irishman kicked back in a lawn chair, sound asleep. He tapped him on the shoulder and the Irishman burst forward out of the chair.

"Bit early isn't it?"

"Yeah, grab your shit. Maybe that lawn chair, if you've grown attached to it."

"Nah, we already got a few in the truck." The Irishman stood up and kicked the chair over.

Thin lines of smoke curled from the embers of last night's fire. Beyond the smoke, a bunkhouse door opened and Logan emerged.

"Where's the rest of your moonshine?" the Irishman asked.

Logan spit to the ground and ran a hand through his long, greasy hair. "What you got to trade for it?"

"How bout your life?"

Logan reached into his pocket for his tiny handgun. The Irishman snapped him in the face with a right hook, sending him to the ground. He kicked the tiny pistol from Logan's hand.

"Stupid asshole." The Irishman bent down and scooped up the pistol.

Trevor heard the confrontation and busted out of the bunkhouse running. The Irishman pocketed the handgun and raised his fists. Trevor stopped dead in his tracks when he saw his buddy laid out on the dirt with a bloody lip.

"Where's the booze?"

Trevor pointed to the bunkhouse he came from.

"Figures. You want to grab that for me?"

Trevor stood still with a dumb look on his face.

"Or you want me to start breaking bones?" The Irishman spit on Logan, who groaned.

"Just get it," Logan said.

It took a minute, but Trevor returned with a milk crate full of mason jars. Half of them were empty. The Irishman turned to Garret. "You want to carry that? I'm still sore."

"Whatever."

Garret grabbed the crate from Trevor. Cody, Alyssa, their Mom, and Malcolm all saw the altercation, but stayed silent as they walked away to load the cars.

Logan pushed himself off the ground.

"Where are you going, Cody?" he asked.

"We're leaving."

"What are we supposed to do?" Logan asked as he wiped blood from his face.

Cody shrugged and gave his sister a light push forward. Garret walked with them to the truck and police cruiser to help them pack, leaving Trevor and Logan with the Irishman.

"You assholes showed up two days ago, and it all went to hell," Logan said.

"Looks like you fought real hard to protect it," the Irishman said.

"Nothing we could do. Now what are we supposed to do?"

"Here." The Irishman pulled the derringer from his pocket. He pulled the slide back five times, ejecting shells. Once the gun was empty, he tossed two rounds to Logan and then the gun.

"One for each of you."

The fuel tanker sat behind a fence next to a brick factory building. A handful of corpses wandered around between the truck and the fence. No telling how many could be in the building. Garret noted the dozens of shot-up rotting bodies on the ground leftover from Crawford's previous fill-ups.

Garret watched as Maps climbed on top of a small shack next to the fence to observe the perimeter through the scope on his rifle.

"Doesn't look too bad. Could be more inside," Garret said. Maps nodded and slung the rifle back over his shoulder. Together, they descended the hill back to their parked vehicles.

"You fellas get a good vantage point?" Malcolm asked.

"Yeah, it doesn't look like there are over six or seven corpses walking around in there. Anyone know how to operate the tanker and release the valve? Hopefully, there is a hose already attached." Garret turned to Jake and Alyssa. "You two are going to help fill up these cans."

The two kids nodded.

"Malcolm, you stay with Janice to watch our rides."

"No." Malcolm stepped forward. "I'm not some useless old man."

"O.K." Garret turned to the Irishman. "Sit this one out."

The Irishman grunted. Good enough.

"Alright everyone, keep quiet. Try not to shoot anything. We don't want to attract more of them. Maps you good?" Garret asked.

Maps nodded and pulled the knife from its sheath.

"Let's go," Garret said.

As they approached the fence, the smell of rotting flesh wafted through the air. The pungent fume assaulted their noses. Malcolm stopped to heave up the little food in his stomach and covered his mouth and nose.

Garret tapped Malcolm on his shoulder and asked, "You okay?"

Malcolm waved the night stick forward, a hand still covering his mouth. "Guess you never get used to that smell."

The front fence swayed open from a light breeze. Garret led the way inside. The group stuck close behind him. Maps broke off to the right to deal with the three dead that were now aware of their presence. Without wasting a second, Garret bee-lined toward the tanker. Malcolm stayed at his side as four corpses shambled in their direction.

A dead construction worker in a bright orange reflective vest dragged his snapped ankle behind him. Malcolm's nightstick bounced off the monster's hard hat. It grabbed him. The monster's furious breath stung Malcolm's eyes.

Garret pulled the zombie off Malcolm and pushed the creature to the ground. He stood on top of it, kicked its hard hat off, and bashed its head in with his brick hammer.

"Thanks." Malcolm readied himself for a husky truck driver. He swung the nightstick, but the creature ducked and fell back. It formed a wall with a brown-haired woman missing half of her scalp and an old skinny woman whose tight flesh outlined her bony skeletal frame. The three corpses stopped their advancement, holding a line.

"The hell are they doing?" Malcolm's mouth dropped open.

"Keep back, something's not right." Garret raised his weapon and met eyes with the skeletal woman. Its pupils shuttered open. The two creatures at his side spread wider, as if they were forming a net.

Ten yards behind them, Cody played with levers and valves on the fuel tanker. Alyssa covered his back with a nine millimeter handgun, ready for any surprise. Maps dropped the last corpse on his side. Jake jumped up and down anxiously with two empty red gas cans in his hands.

"These levers aren't doing anything," Cody said. The sun's glare blocked his eyes from seeing the hose coiled on top of the tanker like a cobra spiraled in its nest.

"Up top," Jake said.

Cody climbed the tanker. He grabbed the hose and lowered one end into a hole in the tank. Once secured, he jumped back down and grabbed a gas can from Jake. He put the hose to his lips and pulled with his lungs. Warm gasoline tasted like fire. He coughed and spit as he filled the first can.

"I got the one on the right." Malcolm walked forward. For each step Malcolm took, the corpses mirrored him in a backward pattern. "They're scared."

Garret didn't move. The world around him slowed down, his mind ticking like a wristwatch. The corpses' behavior didn't add up."Malcolm get back!"

But Malcolm had already committed to another swing with his night-stick. It failed to connect. The creatures continued to retreat, falling back to a row of eighteen wheelers.

Garret dashed to catch up to Malcolm as a corpse dropped from underneath the eighteen wheeler. The chalk white corpse scurried out across the hot pavement on all fours. Black eyes stood out from its powdery white face. A guttural howl exploded out of its throat. More dropped from the other trailers. They had been hiding. Waiting. Patience, a trait Garret didn't know they had.

"Fall back, goddamnit!" Garret yelled.

Malcolm backed away as a line of bodies appeared from the other side of the trucks. The chalky spider zombie answered Malcolm's retreat with a head-on charge. Malcolm bashed the speedy bastard in the face, sending him to the ground. But the black-eyed monster caught itself on the asphalt and regained its balance.

Garret holstered his hammer on his tool belt. So much for quick and easy. Garret snapped the pistol up and fired a round into the zombie's shoulder. It slowed the corpse for a second, enough time for Malcolm to fall back another few feet. The dozens of dead spread apart.

"They're trying to get us in a net. Cody, hurry!" Garret shouted.

Cody finished filling a second five-gallon can, moving onto the next one.

Glass shattered behind the tanker trailer. Maps ran to Garret's side. He spotted a mass of zombies crawling out of the truck stop's broken windows. The truck stop door dinged open as a line of corpses strode outside.

Maps raised the bolt-action rifle to his shoulder, put a target in his scope, and fired. The shot dropped a trucker and put a hole the size of a baby's fist into the chest of the monster behind it.

In a snap, Maps racked the bolt and blasted a second corpse in the head. Like a greased piece of machinery, his arm repeated the action in between shots until the gun was empty. He snatched a handful of rounds from his pocket and quickly chambered them. As Maps unleashed another dose of rifle fire, the headless corpses fell into a pile, temporarily halting the flow of monsters out the front door.

Five abominations made it through the broken windows, shards of glass stuck in their hands and legs as they rushed towards Maps. In between shots, Maps counted at least twenty more threats in the building. He slung the rifle on his back. Maps retrieved a pistol from his shoulder holster and a knife from its sheath.

The white zombie leapt within inches of Garret. At such a close distance, Garret finally landed a headshot. Meanwhile, Malcolm bashed away at the corpses surrounding him, trying to stand his ground. Garret ran up to assist him. Three lay dead at his feet, but they kept coming, one after another.

Cody finished filling the last jug full of gas. "Okay, I'm done." Cody looked up to see the truck yard swarming with monsters. Over ten of the bastards blocked off the way they came through.

"We're getting boxed in!" Cody yelled.

Jake and Alyssa were the only ones able to hear him over the constant rain of gunfire. Cody watched Maps on the frontline, mag dumping a pistol into the truck stop. From behind the tanker, Cody popped out with his assault rifle raised, firing into the horde.

Maps rolled underneath the gas tanker trailer. A corpse tried to follow him, but Maps crushed the monster's head against the pavement with his boot. Garret and Malcolm fell back to the group amidst the chaos.

"Head to the exit. Cover each other," Garret said.

"There's a load of 'em blocking our way out." Cody looked at the ever massing crowd of corpses.

"It was a fucking trap," Garret said.

"How did Crawford manage that?" Malcolm asked.

"He didn't."

They pushed forward in a circle formation. Cody took his time and fired precise shots with his assault rifle. Maps knelt down and pulled a handful of .308 shells from his pocket. Faster than a coin dispenser, Maps loaded the hunting rifle. By the time Garret could line up a kill shot, Maps had already killed another five and bent back down for a quick five shell reload.

"Our left," Malcolm said, and threw a monster to the ground.

An old woman with white hair stained red by blood lashed her arms out. He knew her from before. She used to work at the supermarket. While Malcom hesitated, Cody put an exit wound through her head.

"Don't hesitate again," Cody said to Malcolm. Malcolm nodded.

Quickly, the zombies surged around them. A giant bastard of a monster charged forward, catching Cody by surprise. The monster pinned Cody to the ground by his throat. Saliva drooled past its sharp teeth, dripping onto Cody's cheeks. Desperate for air, Cody choked as he pressed both hands against the monster's neck, trying to push it off. But the big bastard was too heavy.Fingernails sunk into Cody's flesh as it tightened its grip. Cody's eyes bulged.

Alyssa dropped her two gas cans to the ground and whipped the pistol from her holster. She drew a bead on the monster's head and fired. The creature became dead weight, allowing Cody to roll out from under him.

The group went from moving forward at a snail's pace to being frozen in a last stand. Nowhere to retreat as the barrage of corpses sandwiched them between the front entrance and the truck stop. Garret could see more corpses climbing over the fence to their flank.

"There's too many." Garret stated the obvious, but nobody heard him over the screams and gunfire.

Maps stood before an oncoming crowd of frenzied corpses, both guns empty with no time to reload. He held a hunting knife and sunk into a close quarters combat stance.

A runner led the pack with an open mouth that emitted a terrible screeching noise. Maps readied the blade and made eye contact with the rusher.But the monster changed its path at the last second, dodged past Maps, and headed straight for Jake in the center of the group.

Garret tackled the creature to the ground before it could touch the kid. The monster thrashed wildly on the ground against Garret. Its screeching pierced through the sky. Garret straddled the monster, unable to kill it, struggling to keep it pressed to the ground. Malcolm struck the monster across the side of its head with his nightstick. Its screaming trailed off, blood running out of its eyes. Another swing of the nightstick stifled the scream permanently. A jet of black blood oozed across the asphalt.

"Stick tight," Garret shouted. But inside Garret knew they were going to die. The mass of dead collapsed on them from all sides.

Maps fought three corpses at once. He stabbed an obese woman in the side of her head; she fell backwards taking his knife with her. Maps charged two corpses, both trying to grab him at once. He ducked low, tripped one to the ground, and ended it with the heel of his boot. The last one slipped on the slick ground, breaking its teeth on the asphalt. Maps crushed its skull against the pavement. Maps shoved another to the ground and retrieved his knife from the woman's face.

A truck sped through the front fence, breaking through a line of dead. The Irishman leaned out the driver's window with his sawed-off shotgun and blasted away into the herd until he was empty.

"Pass me a gun!" he yelled.

Janice sat in the truck's bed with her hand on a pistol. She held the gun sideways; the barrel pointed at the Irishman.

"Quick," the Irishman said.

Janice saw her two children surrounded. She passed the gun through the back window to the Irishman. The Irishman leaned out his window and started picking off the corpses that remained between the survivors and the truck.

Garret and Maps led the group forward as an unending horde chased after them, tight on their asses.

"Get in!"

Maps helped Jake and Alyssa climb into the truck with the gas cans. Cody hopped in the passenger seat. Garret fired his last bullet, winging an ear off a zombie, and joined Maps in the truck.

As Malcolm grabbed the side of the truck to hop in, an icy hand grabbed his ankle, pulling him down. He kicked. Teeth tore into his calf. Cody grabbed Malcolm's arm, trying to pull him in the truck like a sick game of tug of war. Malcolm opened his mouth to scream, but another pair of hands latched on to his legs. Malcolm's hand slipped through Cody's as the monsters pulled him underneath the truck.

Garret stood up, looking over the side of the truck, ready to jump out to help Malcolm. Maps grabbed him by the shoulder and pulled him back to safety.

"He's dead."

Malcolm screamed under the vehicle. The Irishman put the truck in reverse and slammed his foot on the pedal. The truck bumped over Malcolm and the corpses underneath it, crushing them together as the truck tore out backwards, away from the horde. Their howls chased after them as they tore out onto the road.

Garret stared back at the massive pile of flesh feasting on Malcolm. Those that didn't get a piece lunged after the truck, their black eyes filled with hunger.

23

MAPS PULLED the truck behind Big Jim's Fireworks. Cody followed behind in the police cruiser with his family. A banner featuring a hillbilly riding a rocket hugged the front of the store. Nobody had said much for the two hundred and forty-mile ride. By Maps estimation they were still eight hundred miles shy of their destination. A long way off, and it still felt like death was nipping at their heels.

Garret had hoped for a change of scenery, but Tennessee looked the same as everywhere else, lifeless and abandoned. At least the fireworks shop offered some cheer for Jake and Alyssa, who wouldn't stop bothering Cody to take them inside. He finally gave in once they set up camp; which included a meager fire and a few lawn chairs sitting behind the building.

The Irishman cooked a can of beanie weenies as he sipped on a jar of moonshine.

"Get a can of corn," he said to Maps.

Maps turned to Garret.

"Alright, fine," Garret said, then sighed as he got up. He walked over to the police cruiser, where Janice was sitting in the backseat next to a bag of food. Garret bent down and leaned closer to the open cruiser window.

"Hey, we are cooking if you're hungry. Might want to come out before it's all gone."

Janice offered no response. She just stared straight through the windshield at the red wooden building.

"I'm sorry for your loss. I didn't really know Malcolm, but he seemed like a good man."

A tear rolled down her cheek. Finally, she made eye contact with Garret and said, "He was a good man. Not like you and your men." Her eyes widened. She grabbed Garret by his arm and hissed, "Your friend is the devil!"

Garret broke from her stare and turned his head to see the Irishman laugh and take another sip of shine. He pulled her hand off his arm.

"I need that bag," he said.

Janice shuffled her feet and retrieved the bag. She handed it over, staring off into space.

"Thanks." Garret retrieved a can of corn and walked back to the fire.

"What did she have to say?" the Irishman asked.

"Nothing much."

"She gives me the fucking creeps. Something ain't right when a person don't eat."

"Maps doesn't eat much," Garret said.

"Yeah, and look at him. The slender bastard is the definition of creepy."

Maps shrugged, his nose deep in a book of street maps, plotting their course.

Jake and Alyssa ran around from the side of the building with boxes of fireworks in their hands. Cody rounded the corner next.

"Don't set those off," Garret said.

"They're just sparklers," Cody said as he tossed Jake a lighter.

Jake pulled two out of the box, lit one, and handed it to Alyssa, who ran off to show her mom. Jake lit one for himself and trailed his name in the air.

Garret envied they could forget about where they were and what lurked in the woods all around them. He replayed the morning over in his mind as he ate a spoonful of corn, for which his stomach thanked him. Today wasn't right. The monsters operated with a sense of coordination, like they weren't just a bunch of stupid, hungry corpses.

Stars dimly lit the night. Cody took first watch. The young man climbed up to the roof, where he had an open view of the road and woods surrounding them. The Irishman sipped his moonshine like it was a fine wine, savoring every ounce of the harsh flavor. Alyssa and Jake sat in the dirt, sharing a peanut butter protein bar.

"I didn't want to say it, but those monsters are getting smarter," Garret said.

"You just now figured that out?" the Irishman said and leaned forward. "Two months ago they weren't jumping around and setting traps. Shit, they weren't even moving together in groups besides in the cities."

"Who thought the dead could think?" Garret said.

"First few months they sure as hell didn't."

A silence trickled over the camp. It was quiet enough that they could hear a mosquito fart.

"Do you have video games at your house?" Jake asked.

"No, but I've got the next best thing --"

"Movies?" Jake interrupted.

"Oh. No, but I have a lot of books," Garret said.

Jake sighed and went back to eating the expired protein bar. The air had a sudden chill in it. The car door cracked open. Janice stepped out with a knife in her hand.

"What's this crazy bitch doing now?" the Irishman asked.

"They're coming. I heard their whispers in the woods," Janice said. Her hand tightened around the knife.

Garret jumped out of the lawn chair and walked toward the woods. The hill behind their camp dipped down to what looked like a creek, but it was near impossible to tell what was lurking down there from the thick brush. He didn't doubt that there were dead in the woods. But they would have heard twigs snap and smelled them if they approached the camp.

"Put the knife down before you hurt yourself, woman," the Irishman said.

"Shh," Garret said. He cupped a hand over his ear and walked closer to the woods. He listened to the buzz of insects and crickets chirping. A breeze rustled the tree branches.

"I hear nothing," Garret said.

"Cause this bitch is crazy," the Irishman said.

"Don't call her that," Cody called down from atop the roof.

The Irishman finished the jar of moonshine and tossed it into the fire. Glass shattered. He pushed himself off the lawn chair and struggled to stand. He swayed to the left and the right; the taste of gasoline lingered on his taste buds.

"It's too dark to see anything down there," Garret said.

"Give me the knife," the Irishman said.

"Mom, put it down," Alyssa chimed in.

Janice backed away from the Irishman, the knife still glued to her hand.

The Irishman burped fire as he walked toward Janice. He cornered her against the car. She held the knife tucked in close to her chest. He opened his palm for her to hand him the blade. Darkness made the Irishman look deranged with his dirty clothes and blood stained eye patch as he swayed back and forth.

Garret thought he saw a shadow move in the woods. But he couldn't tell if it was just a bird or a branch moving in the wind. He stepped into the untamed grass. A few feet from where he stood, the ground curved down into a valley of fiendish looking trees. Their branches resembled arms trying to pull Garret in. A sense of dread poured out of the woods, infesting Garret.

"Stop it," Cody said as he slung the rifle over his shoulder and climbed down off the roof.

"Hand it over," the Irishman said.

"Get away from me!" Janice yelled. She slashed the knife through the air in front of her.

The Irishman leaned back far enough to dodge the attack. Then leapt forward on his drunk feet and snatched her wrist. He twisted her wrist back until she cried out in pain and dropped the knife to the dirt before letting her go.

Janice slapped him hard across the face, drawing blood from his lip. The Irishman stood still in a drunken stupor, prodding his fattened lip with his index finger.

"Bastard," she said, and slapped him again.

The Irishman backhanded her across the face, sending her tumbling backwards against the police cruiser. Janice fell down to her knees.

"Fuck," the Irishman said. He dabbed his lip again and turned around.

Cody dropped his rifle to the ground and charged at the Irishman. Their bodies collided, catching the brute by surprise and taking him to the dirt.

"Don't you ever fucking touch her again."

Cody punched the Irishman in the face, tearing his busted lip open. Blood streaked down the Irishman's chin as Cody struck him again. The Irishman blocked the third punch and hit Cody square in the gut. Cody fell off him, landing to his side, gasping for air.The two of them lay collapsed in the dirt.

Eventually the Irishman pushed himself off the ground and wiped his dirt covered palms off on his jeans. On his way back to the lawn chair he almost tripped, but caught himself.

Cody cooled off on the dirt, recollecting the air that had been knocked out of him. He rolled over and stood up. Behind him, Janice sat against the car, crying.

"He's the devil, he's the devil," she mumbled again and again.

Cody held her head against his shoulders. Janice stared into the Earth and repeated her chant. "He's the devil, he's the devil."

Jake and Alyssa's sparklers hung limp by their sides.

The Irishman hawked a crimson ball of saliva to the ground and reclined back in his lawn chair.

Maps walked to the edge of the hill next to Garret with a flashlight in hand. He flicked it on and shined the light into the woods below them. A maze of twisted trees wrapped around each other and blocked the bottom of the forest. The light stopped on a single man standing in the woods. He wore a hat with his head low, blocking the sight of his face. A gash split open the front of his knee, revealing a combination of dirtied muscles and tendons.

"I don't think he's alive," Garret said.

Maps continued to sweep the woods with light. He stopped on a wide tree trunk and pointed at it with his free hand. But Garret couldn't see it.

He stepped closer for a better angle and saw a shoulder behind the bark that nearly blended into the tree. Maps turned the light back to the man in the baseball cap. His murky eyes bounced the light back at Garret and Maps.

"What's going on?" Jake asked. Then he saw the monster basking in the spotlight, staring at him, baring its disjointed teeth. Jake froze.

"Get in the truck," Maps said.

Jake ran back to the truck. Maps shifted the light and pointed to another corpse peeking out from behind a log, its bony fingers dug into the bark.

"They're watching us," Garret said.

Maps raised the light up through the treetops above them. The beaming light exposed a dozen eyes in the mess of leaves and branches.

"I count fifteen." Garret backed up from the hill. "Probably more in the trees we can't see."

"Why aren't they attacking?" Cody asked.

"We need to go." Garret walked away from Maps, who was still staring the monsters down.

"But I'm just feeling nice and buzzed." The Irishman cradled the back of his head in his palms. "Let them come up the hill."

Maps flicked off the flashlight and walked away from the edge of the hill. Whatever the hell they were up to wasn't good. Maybe it was a trap or a distraction for a flank. Nobody was on the roof watching the other side of the road and building.

"You can still drink. Just put that lawn chair in the back of the truck," Garret said.

"Fine." The Irishman stood up and grabbed Maps by the shoulder. "Want me to drive?"

Maps shook his head.

Leaves rustled in the brush behind the makeshift camp. Maps threw the backpack into the truck and hopped into the driver's seat.

"Garret, ride with them," the Irishman said, his eyes on Janice and Alyssa as they squeezed into the backseat of the cruiser.

"Sure."

Before they departed, Garret helped the Irishman finish loading the truck.

"You don't trust them," Garret said.

"If you do, then you're as dumb as I thought. You miss the kid hitting me? That bastard wouldn't have stopped unless I made him. And his mom is a ticking time bomb. Crawford walks amongst the dead and her head's still full of his nut job ideologies."

"She's scared, and I can't blame her. I'm scared too. But they wouldn't take half our supplies and run."

The Irishman grunted and turned his gaze to the forest. "Your tendency to save everyone is going to get us killed."

Garret ignored the remark. He wouldn't turn his back on Cody. The Irishman couldn't have hated the kid too much or Cody wouldn't have been able to walk after swinging against the Irishman.

"Come on, let's go," Cody said.

Their brights swallowed Garret whole, blinding him as he got into the passenger seat. They followed close behind the truck in front of them. In minutes, Alyssa and her mom passed out in the back. Too much excitement for one day. Garret wished those damn monsters hadn't been in the woods. Pure exhaustion set in. He tilted his head against the window, ready to pass out.

"How did you link up with them?" Cody asked.

Garret snapped forward, wondering why the kid was asking him about this now. "Uh, it's sort of a crazy story. Why do you ask?"

"Figured we could shoot the shit, so I don't fall asleep behind the wheel here."

"That's it?"

"Not really. I mean, you're not like them, Garret. Complete opposites, actually. I got a feeling they didn't want us tagging along at all."

"You're not wrong. They might be a little harsh around the edges, but underneath they're decent people. At least that's what I tell myself. There's no doubt in my mind I'd be dead without them. Honestly, I just want to see my family again. And I'd do anything to make that happen."

"I guess that makes sense."

They sat in silence for a good part of an hour, trailing behind the truck in front of them. Trees blurred by their side as Garret nodded off.

"Hey, Garret?" Cody yawned.

Still half-asleep, Garret opened his eyes. "Yeah? What is it?"

"Mind telling me that story? I just caught myself drifting off."

"Sure, it all started in a mall in Florida."

24

GARRET RAN FAST AGAIN like he used to on the school's track before fifteen years of marriage, beer, and barbecue. A bullet whizzed past his head and crashed into a cardboard cutout of a giant smoothie. Garret made a sharp right into the mall's food court. Five minutes prior he'd ran into two survivors that looked nice enough, but as soon as they saw him the two assholes chased him. Had everyone lost their minds?

He slipped into a massive pool of crimson fluid. His ass hit the porcelain tile hard. Shoes squeaked as Garret slid into the body of a decrepit man with a hole in his forehead.

"Son--" Jones gasped deep for air, "Son-of-bitch." He panted, hammer at his side as his friend Vlad, carrying a handgun, caught up with him.

Vlad wiped sweat from his brow with a wicked smile. He raised the handgun up.

"Got you," Vlad said.

Jones observed the food court.

Dizzy and nauseous, Garret tried to stand but lost footing, this time ending up on his stomach. He saw the food court in its entirety. Enough bodies lay on the ground to fill every chair, holes in each of their heads. A man sat at a table in the center of the food court, eating frozen yogurt with a power drill in his lap. He wore an ugly palm tree patterned Hawaiian shirt, the price tag still hung on its side. He had a grizzled, carefree look to him.

Garret sat up against the corpse, finding his footing in the bloody mess.

"Hey friend, share some of that," Vlad said. The Russian took a step forward. If he was afraid, he didn't show it.

The man at the table licked his spoon and set the cup of frozen yogurt down. He lifted the power drill out of his lap and aimed it like a gun, his finger on the trigger.

"That's close enough. We didn't risk our lives to turn on the generator so you could fuck with my dessert."

Vlad laughed and took another step, still twenty-five yards away.

"What are you going to do with that?" Vlad waved his handgun.

"I modified this power drill to shoot .308. Wanna see?"

"Vlad, let's go. This guy doesn't have jack shit," Jones said.

"Bullshit."

"Vlad, I'm being sincere when I say this. If you can't shoot me from that distance then truly you're fucked."

Vlad raised the pistol. A bullet snapped his skull back against his shoulders. Jones turned to run, the rifle shot still echoing through the mall.

Garret watched as the man lowered the power drill and took another bite of his melting, frozen yogurt. A second shot boomed through the mall. Jones' body became a rag doll and tumbled into the dry fountain with a resounding thud.

A hollow man in blue jeans walked out from behind a counter with a hot cinnamon roll and a hunting rifle slung on his back. He sat down across from the man with the power drill.

Garret got up off the decrepit corpse once he was pretty sure they wouldn't kill him, too. Blood soaked the front and back of his clothes. His hands stuck to his shorts as he attempted to wipe it off before it crusted to his skin.

"Thanks, uh, you guys. You saved me. My name's Garret."

"Where are your weapons?" The man finished his yogurt.

"I don't have any. Excuse me, uh, what's your name?"

"We don't do names."

"O.K." Garret paused, unsure of what to say next. The man had a hard look to him. Garret focused on his breathing in case he needed to run again.

"I waved down this car. They started chasing me and shooting at me. So I ran into the mall, I thought I could--"

"You waved down a car without weapons?" The man held the spoon in front of his smile to cover his laughter.

"Go ahead, take a seat," he said.

Garret sat down at the table across from the man with the power drill. Tiny specks of blood littered the yellow table top.

"I try to avoid that type of conflict."

"Garret you got your thinking cap on backwards." He pointed his spoon to the fresh bodies. "That is survival."

"I appreciate you guys saving me, but that seemed unnecessary."

"A few nights ago we were hiking on some ass backwards path to skip a high density area. An old hiking trail with a few campsites. We heard somebody playing a guitar and we could hear conversation. We smelled the smoke of their fire and thought, shit maybe we can get a meal. So we scoped it out, and we saw this old couple. Grandpa strummed the guitar while the grandma stirred a pot. Such a wonderful smelling stew. So we get closer and then we see it. Half of a man strapped to a table, limbs missing. Pieces of his body were rolled in salt, splayed out in front of him. You could tell from the lines on his face that he was scared when he died, and that he died slowly."

The man stopped the story and flicked his spoon to the ground.

"What happened?"

"We shot them. When we searched their camp we found a rifle, jugs of water, and a stocked pantry. How long had it been? Two weeks?"

The thin man nodded. But he was more invested in the meticulous unraveling of his Cinnamon roll.

"Two weeks and these assholes were already eating people. Maybe I could see it if grandma and grandpa were starving and hiker Billy broke his neck. So fine, eat Billy to survive. But they had a full fucking pantry. Poor Billy probably thought they looked innocent, tried to share a meal, got his head bashed in instead and cut apart like he was cattle."

"So you murdered them?"

"Yeah, killed them both before they knew we were there. But you know what? We didn't fucking eat them."

Death meant nothing to them. No remorse had surfaced on either man's face at any point during the tale. They scared Garret more than the monsters that had just been chasing him. Yet he remained seated across from the Grim Reaper and his skinny pal. The fading sunlight made the food court look more like a morgue rather than a destination for swirly ice cream cones and bad Chinese.

Maps devoured the cinnamon roll and licked his fingers. He eyed the shadows growing across the floor, spreading like a disease up the walls. He looked at his wrist as if he were wearing a watch.

"Aye." The man grabbed his power drill, stood up and said, "Good luck."

Garret watched as the thin man followed his friend's departure. Besides the power drill, all they had were two backpacks and a bolt-action rifle. Alone and surrounded by bodies, Garret lightly tapped his fingers on the table. Outside, he could hear the faint moaning of the dead. His legs burned and feet ached. How much further would he have to run? His fingers hit the table hard now, in rhythm with his thoughts.

The power drill sounded more like a blender inside of the monster's skull. Garret watched the brute grab one by its throat and then rammed the drill through its head. He covered his ears as he approached them from behind.

Maps turned around with the butt of his rifle tucked in his shoulder. Garret threw his hands in the air. The corpse hit the floor, and the man with the drill turned around.

"You got more people chasing you?" he asked.

"No, where are you guys headed?"

"South to the gulf. We'll find a yacht with a bar and sail off somewhere. Not that it's any of your business," he said as he picked pieces of brain from the drill head.

Garret shrugged and said, "You're too late for that."

The man looked up from his drill with a soured face. "What are you saying?"

"I stayed holed up in my hotel room for the first two weeks, hoping the situation would cool off or the military would resolve it. On the third day of this shit storm they broadcasted a helicopter flying over the coast. There wasn't a single boat at the docks. I flipped through channels and saw the same thing in Miami, Tallahassee, and New Orleans. You'd be lucky to find a canoe full of holes," Garret said.

"Fuck you, we'll find a boat."

"Maybe you will. But I'm headed to my fortress in Pennsylvania. It's stocked with canned food, a gas generator, and a fully stocked bar. Though the limes may have gone brown by now."

"Bullshit, someone probably raided it," he said.

"No, that's just what's in the bunker. And my wife's the survivalist type. I know she's still alive, holding down the base," Garret said with a smile.

"No, thanks. We've already come this far."

"I'm telling you, you won't find any boats," Garret lied.

"Maybe we should take our chances."

"Yeah, take your chances with me."

Garret watched as the Irishman took a swig straight from a bottle of vodka.

"I've got Scotch, whiskey, gin, wine and way better vodka than what you're drinking now. We'll be safe there, I promise."

The brute stopped mid-step and turned to his slender friend, who shrugged.

"You got a coin?"

"Uh, hold on a second." Garret searched his pockets, knowing he didn't bring any change on this journey.

"Wait," Garret said and rushed over to the fountain, returning with a quarter.

"Heads or tails?" the brute asked.

Garret flipped the coin.

25

As the convoy approached a bridge, they slowed to a stop just yards from a compact road with only two lanes. A wall of zombies occupied the other side of the bridge. The monsters turned their heads in unison. They basked in the halogen light from the cruiser's headlights. Alyssa leaned out of the back passenger's side window of the cruiser with a spotlight.

The Irishman rolled down the window, turned his head back to the cruiser and shouted, "We kill them fast and drive on!"

Maps got out of the truck, a knife already in his hand. He walked around and tapped the hood of the cruiser while everyone else followed suit.

At the front of the mob, a zombie that towered over the others charged forward. It swung its head wildly as it got closer to its food source. The group of survivors formed a line.

"There's too many. We should turn around. Looks like someone tried to blow this bridge apart with explosives," Cody said.

Garret nodded. Directly in the middle of the bridge was a massive hole. Their vehicles would need to hug either side to have a chance of getting past.

"We go forward." The Irishman stepped down out of the truck, holding a shotgun in his hands. He quickly checked the chamber and positioned himself in a shooting stance.

"This is a bad idea." Cody pressed the butt of his rifle into his shoulder.

Garret held a hammer with a pistol tucked into his waistband. The monsters were close enough that the air smelled of rotting flesh and sour milk. Garret wished for a mask to cover his face, or at least a clothespin to bind his nose shut.

"Hit the big guy first," Garret said.

The Irishman couldn't draw a bead on the football player's head. The corpse swayed his pock-marked face randomly to the left and right.

Garret turned to Jake before they turned the road into chaos and said, "Watch our flank."

"Okay," Jake said. He climbed into the back of the truck to watch the empty road behind them.

The Irishman gave up on a headshot. He pulled the trigger, releasing a spread of pellets that dismantled the chest cavity of the hulking monster. The creature fell backward from the force of the blast, but recovered thanks to a push from one of his dead comrades.

Cody rattled off a few bursts of his rifle. With each round of rifle fire, he thinned the front line of approaching corpses. Each body he dropped was replaced by another.

"There are more across the bridge in the woods," Cody said.

The towering corpse missing half of its chest charged straight toward them. The Irishman swung the shotgun low and removed the monster's kneecaps with a second blast, sending the monster face forward into the pavement.

The gap between the tide of creatures on the bridge and the challenging convoy shrank. Garret fired a magazine of nine millimeter rounds, killing only three or four of the damned beasts. The rest of his shots created non-lethal flesh wounds, barely slowing their approach.

Next to Garret, Alyssa stood in a wide stance. She fired each round with a sense of methodical care. Though she shot slowly, almost every bullet destroyed a brain or spine.

A small mound of bodies piled up in the middle of the bridge. Their numbers thinned thanks to a constant barrage of gunfire. Great, we've almost won, Garret thought. Then Jake fired off a round, and Garret turned to their flank. A marathon of corpses paraded around the bend in the road behind their convoy. Garret couldn't see an end to the army behind them.

"We need to finish this fast," Garret yelled.

The Irishman found himself sobered by the impending band of corpses threatening to sandwich them. He loaded three shells in the shotgun and pushed forward onto the bridge. Maps did the same, with only a knife in his hand. Buckshot tore through multiple brains at a time.

Maps rampaged across the bridge with his blade. A female in a sports bra and sleek running pants dashed across the bridge. Mud matted patches of her blond hair together and a gaping hole in her cheek exposed broken yellow teeth.

Maps tried to stab her in the face, but she caught the knife through her right hand, stopping the blade from reaching her skull. Maps wrestled with her to pull the stuck blade from her bony palm. She reached her neck out with her jaw gaping open, trying to find flesh, but Maps maneuvered backward, dragging her with him to the side of the bridge. He shoved her into the violent river below, his knife still stuck in her hand.

"Only three more shells," the Irishman said. He loaded them in quick succession. As fast as he loaded the shotgun, he spent the ammo on the remaining stragglers. Only a thin mob of dead remained to their front. The rest of the corpses lay strewn across the cracked pavement. A strong wind slightly swayed the bridge to the left.

"Shit, this structure's barely standing. Can we even drive over it?" Garret asked.

"We have to try or we're dead here."

An endless herd of zombies closed the gap from behind. Everyone hurried back into their vehicles. Garret drove the truck with Jake in the back. Bodies crunched under its wheels as they hugged the right side of the bridge. In the rear-view mirror the cruiser followed them along with a parade of corpses. Rotted arms lashed out, hitting the back of the police cruiser.

In the middle of the bridge, Maps stomped the brains out of a straggler.

The remaining four monsters growled and barked like wild wolves as they retreated into the woods. The Irishman looked over the side at the thirty-foot drop into the raging water below. A deep crack split down the side of the concrete support. He swallowed a lump in his throat as the truck pulled up next to him. The Irishman jumped onto the side of the truck and leaned through the rolled-down window.

"Drive. It won't hold."

The bridge swayed as the monsters chased after them. Bodies of brained corpses lay on the bridge as speed bumps, preventing either vehicle from going more than a few miles per hour. They felt the bridge sway to the right. Everyone dead and alive on the bridge heard a cracking sound from underneath.

Garret slammed his foot on the pedal, but the road in front of them split in two. Garret pumped the brakes and stopped as the pavement crumbled and the support beneath them gave way. The concrete rapidly fractured. It felt as if their entire world slid at a 45-degree angle. Garret turned to see the cruiser with Cody and his family drop through the bridge and splash, disappearing into the river below them.

"Fuck," the Irishman said. He held onto the side of the truck as the concrete support beneath them disintegrated.

The bridge shifted, arcing up. Garret's stomach sank. He felt the truck slide backwards. And then he was weightless for a moment. The airbag sprung into Garret's face as the back of the truck broke into the water. Disorientated from the blow, Garret barely noticed water rising above his ankles.

The truck sank fast. Garret tugged at the door handle, but the water pressure prevented it from opening. He climbed over the center console and pulled himself through the passenger's window. The rivers current tried to swallow him. Garret kicked off from the submerged vehicle. His sinuses burned from the invading water.

Garret swam up desperately. He needed air, but the undertow turned him around and yanked him back. For a moment he lost all sense of direction. He saw purple. Nothing else. Lost and helpless. He jerked his arms forward, grasping for anything. Water rushed through his mouth and nose, choking him. A faint glimpse of moonlight shimmered above and he fought. With every bit of energy, he kicked his legs and stroked upward, reaching toward the faint light. At last Garret broke the surface, tasting the night's air.

26

GARRET CHOKED, coughing up the river water. He climbed ashore the bottom of a muddy bank. He saw the Irishman sprawled out where the mud turned to grass, looking at the stars through the leaves of a tree. Further down the bank Cody knelt over Alyssa, pumping breath into her lungs. Janice cried loudly at his side.

Garret eyed the river. No sign of Jake or Maps or their vehicles. Garret examined the crumbled bridge and the hundred monsters standing over the edge, watching them. A forgotten sense of urgency overcame him. Garret ran to the Irishman.

"Did you see Maps or Jake? We've got to help them."

The Irishman sighed. "The kid went under. Disappeared underneath the truck."

"You couldn't get to him?" Garret asked.

"I barely got out myself. Thought you were certainly dead."

"What about Maps?"

The Irishman sat up and pointed to the river. Garret turned around. He saw a figure briefly surface from the water, then dive back under. Over a minute passed before he re-surfaced, then he went under again, continuing the loop.

"The man is an ex-seal. That's what he must be. Otherwise, he would have drowned by now. Never seen someone tangle in that type of water for so long." The Irishman laid back down in the grass.

Garret heard Alyssa choke up water, coming back to life. He watched Cody and Janice hug her as she spit water from her mouth, her eyes wide and unaware of the nightmare she woke back up to.

Maps finally returned from the river, alone. He shook the water from his body, and as usual, he said nothing. An unmistakable sense of sadness spread across his face.

Only some of the dead remained at the end of the bridge. The rest of the crowd had dissipated, most likely trying to find a way down to them that didn't involve a thirty-foot drop into a vicious river.

A numbness fell over Garret. Was he so used to death that he could no longer mourn? Did he forget how? He had barely known Jake. All he could think about was the fear he felt when the current sucked him under. To have water fill your lungs, he thought. The poor boy didn't deserve that. He shivered and wished that he were a stronger man. That he could have saved the boy, or anyone else. When Jake had gotten pulled beneath the truck, Garret had been probably fiddling with his seat belt, maybe recovering from the blow of the airbags. Useless.

"I'm sorry," Garret said.

The apology fell on deaf ears. The Irishman lay half asleep in the grass. Maps was trapped in his own head, stuck staring at the moving river. Garret walked down the bank toward Cody and his family. Cody stepped out of the mud and walked with Garret down the bank.

"What are we going to do?" Cody asked.

"Keep moving. Won't be long before the dead find us."

"We don't have any weapons, or food." Cody shook his head in disappointment. "I thought you were a good leader. It was a mistake. My mistake. We're all going to die, aren't we?"

"I'm a fucking insurance salesman. I never claimed to be your leader. You wanted to travel with us and I vouched for you."

Cody kicked a glob of mud off his shoe into the water. He shoved Garret's arm from his shoulder. Garret could see the young man shivering through the wet clothes.

"I didn't know your friends were like this."

Garret felt insulted. "Like what?"

"One of them is a drunk asshole and the other a mute psychopath. You know what? I take it back, they are both psychos."

"Those two are more dangerous unarmed than us with a whole damn arsenal. They've kept me alive and they'll keep you alive if you aren't a dick."

"That bastard hit my mother," Cody said.

"Let it go Cody."

"Garret, you're an alright guy, but your friends aren't good people."

"I know our situation looks bad." Garret tried to convince Cody to stick with them. He had been in worse situations than this and survived. That's what he would keep doing. He didn't come this damned far to give up now.

"It's worse than bad. We're screwed." Cody was about to say something else when Alyssa walked up to his side.

Alyssa looked at Garret. "Where's Jake?"

Garret felt defeated. The words couldn't come out of his mouth, he just delivered the bad news by shaking his head. Alyssa tried to hold back the tears, but the floodgates opened.

"What happened?" she cried.

"Come on." Cody grabbed her hand and walked her back to their mom.

Garret walked back up the bank to round up Maps and the Irishman. They couldn't afford to think about Jake right now, or they would all join him shortly.

The Irishman was off the ground when Garret returned. Nothing needed to be said. They all knew that they were in for a long walk. Like before. Garret had traveled more miles by foot than any vehicle since this mess started. Of course, having a vehicle to carry supplies was a luxury, but unnecessary. Garret wouldn't say it out loud, but he would rather be on foot, anyway.

Together they all walked about a mile down the river's bank under the moonlight. Garret wanted to say something to bring up the morale of the group, but nothing sounded appropriate in his head. Maybe by the end of the night he would find the proper words. A feeling of emptiness and defeat gnawed at him as they walked.

Alyssa kept taking hopeful glances toward the river, looking for Jake. But in the pit of his stomach, Garret knew he was gone.

"Maybe he got out on the other side," she said.

Garret shook his head and waited, hoping that someone else would tell her otherwise. He figured deep down that she knew what happened to Jake, but she wasn't ready to accept it.

"If he did, he could be looking for us, back where we got out."

"He's gone," Cody said.

The air dried their clothes over the course of two miles. The river narrowed and the mud bank got deep. Each step became a chore. They struggled to keep the marsh from pulling their shoes off their feet. They changed course to a drier path through a dense brush. Branches and thorns scratched their faces, leaves stuck to the mud on their boots.

An array of clouds blocked the moonlight from reaching them. Truth be told, the darkness scared Garret. He could no longer see Maps in front of them. His feet burned, a familiar feeling in which he found comfort. The Irishman walked by his side, spitting as if he were smoking a cigar in his happy place.

After a short trek through the brush, they found a clearing in the woods. Garret stretched his calves as Janice and Alyssa caught up. They took no effort in hiding their exhaustion. Janice breathed heavily, like she finished a marathon through the desert. Alyssa let out an annoyed sigh as she took off her shoes and wet socks.

"Maps?" Garret whispered. A fog smothered the woods with smoky white walls. Dew settled along their bare skin, and Garret recognized his pulse rising.

"Why do you call him that?" Cody asked.

"Because he always knows the way to go," Garret said. But each moment Maps didn't re-appear from the fog, Garret worried more.

"Where did he go then?" Cody asked.

"Ahead. Let's keep moving. He isn't used to waiting on us."

"We need a break," Janice said, her breath still heavy.

Alyssa pinched her socks and held them out in the air. "Five more minutes."

The Irishman slapped a mosquito off his arm. He plucked clumps of wet gauze from his gouged eye with a muddy hand. No sign of pain on his face, just a look of disgust as he pulled out the last of the bloody cotton and discarded it to the ground. Unlovable ugliness. There was an abyss in his eye socket that made him look as lifeless as the dead.

"Let them catch up." The Irishman continued on into the fog.

Garret followed. They survived because they moved. Cody and his family needed a reality check. The three miles they traveled were nothing compared to the hikes they had done before, days of walking without food, blisters that popped, drained, and blistered again. It only took a few minutes for Alyssa to catch up with Cody and Janice trailing behind her.

"Where's the stickman?" Alyssa asked.

"He's fine," the Irishman said.

"How does he have a sense of direction in this? What if he turned back trying to find us and walked right by without knowing?" Cody said.

"Fuck the what ifs. Save your breath and keep walking." The Irishman pushed forward.

They found Maps leaning against a tree, a silhouette in the fog. As the group got closer, they saw a monster pinned to the tree with a knife. It was the same knife that had been lodged in the hand of the monster on the bridge.

"What happened?" Garret asked.

Maps put a finger to his lips, and Garret opened his ears to the night. Beyond the trees and fog, Garret could make out the sound of leaves rustling and distant footsteps.

"They looped around us. So we would walk right into them," Garret said.

Maps pulled the blade from the monster's skull, and the corpse slid down against the tree to the ground. He pointed west to grassy ground that curved up and disappeared behind the fog. It was one hell of an overgrown hill.

If the monsters really tracked them, how did they stand a chance? How can we get away from them if they never stop chasing us? The hope that always lived in Garret slowly faded. Hope that he would make it back home alive, that he could see his wife one last time. But they still had hundreds of miles to go and the dead were thinking and planning. They were learning. Learning fast.

"My knees hurt," Janice said. She was bent over, hands rubbing her knees that had been scrapped up by the crash. Cody grabbed her hand to help guide her.

A distant growl echoed through the fog. It provided an imminent jolt of motivation for everyone. There wouldn't be much of a fight if the dead caught up to them. They would tear them apart, well, except for Maps. Garret bet he would out maneuver them.

Garret could tell Janice was weak. Being able to see weakness had made Garret an excellent insurance sales agent. Though he never thought he would use this skill to determine -- determine what? Janice was slowing them down. That was no secret, but leaving the poor woman behind would condemn Cody and Alyssa to death. Or their resentment would boil to the surface and doom Garret and his group. Garret shook the thoughts from his mind. Focus. Focus on this hill.

The hill was raw and muddy. Thin dead trees had grown at an unusual angle, roots poked out from the Earth. The fog had done a good job at hiding its true steepness. Garret wondered if Maps chose this difficult route on purpose. Maybe Jake's death clouded his judgement. Neither possibility was improbable or good. Garret sighed as he grabbed a root and found better footing.

Garret looked down. Alyssa was right behind him, but the fog blocked him from seeing anything else. A heavy rain broke through the sky, making the already difficult hill a bigger pain.

"How far behind are they?" Garret asked.

"Not far. Cody made me promise him I would beat him to the top."

"Go right ahead," Garret said and welcomed Alyssa past him. He carefully made his way back down the hill. He guessed the hill was slanted at about a 60-degree angle. It was as if they were scaling the side of a mountain, straining their legs. About fifteen yards later, he saw Cody helping Janice move one step at a time. If only he could carry her, Garret thought.

To make things worse, the light rain turned into a full-blown storm. The noxious smell of rotting flesh wafted up from behind Cody and Janice.

"Garret, I can hear them. They're catching up to us," Cody said.

"Let me help."

The sky cracked open with thunder. A lighting bolt cast through the clouds, reducing the opacity of the fog, and Garret saw them. The flash of light revealed a horde of dead working their way up the hill. The hard, skeletal beings crawled up at a rapid pace. In a few minutes, they would catch them. An overwhelming downpour turned the hill into a muddy mess.

Garret helped Cody with Janice, but the rain turned the landscape into brown sludge. Each step became a struggle. It wasn't working. Lightning flashed, showing the dead climbing over their own who got stuck in the Earth. They were getting closer.

The rain poured harder, and Garret slipped forward in the mud. He bashed the front of his face on a branch and almost slid down the hill, desperately clinging to a root.

He regained his balance as he felt the bush giving way to his weight. Garret bent down and pulled off his boots. It was too hard for him to move with them, getting stuck in the mud with every step. He carried them tightly under his arms, mud squishing between his toes. As they neared the peak of the hill, the fog thinned out. Garret could see Maps lending Alyssa a hand, pulling her to the top.

"Almost there," Garret said.

Another bolt of lightning shattered the darkness of the night. A thriving mass of flesh followed them up the muddy slope. A lone corpse spearheaded the ascent, thin patches of skin covered its slender body, the top of its skull bleached by the sun. Despite the beast having no eyes, it could sense them. It climbed faster than the others.

The last five yard stretch was the worst. No roots, trees, or rocks to use to one's advantage, just ground that shifted like pure liquid. Garret found himself stuck, almost knee deep in the mud. When he turned to his side, he found Janice and Cody in the same predicament.

"We could use a fucking hand here!" Garret said, the panic high in his voice.

Maps appeared over the top of the hill. The night lit up again, reflecting the pursuers in Map's eyes, and without hesitation he took the knife in his hand and began his descent.

"Leave me," Janice said to Cody.

Garret shifted one foot at a time, trying to find leverage in the thick dirt soup. He grabbed Janice's hand and pulled her out of the mud, sinking himself deeper. Nobody else would die tonight. He did the same for Cody and felt mud rise above his knees. He could see Maps closing in on him, but not fast enough.

The skeletal corpse towered over Garret. The monster's light, bony feet supported it through the mud. Garret had no weapon except for his hands. He turned his torso as far as it would go and raised his fists. The creature's icy hands grabbed his wrists and with surprising force overpowered Garret.

As the monster pushed his arms down, it leaned forward, mouth wide open, ready to bite. Feeling the skeleton's overwhelming center of gravity on top of him, Garret ripped his right arm free. The movement thrust the zombie's ankle toward him and the bastard lost its balance, sliding down the hill out of control.

Maps reached out his hand, and Garret grabbed it, pulling himself out of the mud. Finally, he made it to the top of the hill. The rain not only hid the sweat on Garret's face and arms, it masked his fear in unison with the night.

They all stood atop the hill, under the storm, looking down at the dead stuck in the mud. They won. The dead couldn't make it any further. Garret laughed at the thought of relating to their frustration, as if they felt frustration or any other emotion other than the desire to eat the living's flesh. For all he could tell, hunger was the only instinct that drove them. Another thing he could relate to, but right now he didn't want to think of all the things they shared in common with the dead. It made the monsters more human. No, that wasn't right. It made humans more monster.

"What's so funny?" the Irishman asked.

"Nothing. They just haven't figured everything out yet."

"No need to wait around for that," the Irishman said.

"Look at them." Cody pointed down to the base of the muddy basin.

The monsters turned on each other. Those stuck close together tore at one another with teeth and their fingernails. Three corpses shoved a fat man to the mud and pulled him apart, sticking pieces of dead flesh into their mouths and chewing viciously.

The downpour eliminated the muggy hotness from the air. Garret appreciated the cooling-off period for a few minutes before he stood up to usher everyone back on the move. They still had miles to walk before daylight.

27

THE SUNRISE MADE Garret think of his wife, Emily. Before he sold insurance, they would often wake up early, brew a pot of coffee, and sit outside together on their deck to watch the night turn to dawn. It had been awhile since he had seen the sunrise, yet it still brought back fond memories. He thought of her less now.

Garret focused on the burning soreness that stretched through his legs with each step forward. They had reached the edge of the woods and were now loosely following a road. Garret trusted Maps' sense of direction, so he didn't bother to ask where they were going. All he knew was that they were still in Tennessee and over six hundred miles away from his destination.

"Break," Garret said and came to a stop at the bottom of a hill.

Exhaustion gripped the group. Garret even saw Maps yawn, and that was something he had never seen the man do before. Janice and Alyssa let out a tired set of breaths. If it wasn't for Cody, Janice wouldn't have made it this far. But how could Garret fault her for being older and unable to keep pace with everyone else?

"I need a drink," the Irishman said.

Garret too wished for hydration, at least enough so he could form the saliva needed to lick his chapped lips. They wouldn't make it much further without water. Food was secondary. Garret worried the afternoon sun would beat them until they were chalk, and Janice would surely have a heat stroke if they kept this pace.

"Maps, where exactly are we?" Garret asked.

Maps lay on the grass, his eyes watching the light blue sky and pillow like clouds. With the sunlight on his face, Garret could see a clear sorrow that he previously couldn't make out in the dark.

"Six miles outside of Celina county," Maps said.

"Celina? Are you kidding me?" The Irishman looked like he wanted to spit to the ground, but lacked the saliva.

"What's in Celina?" Garret asked.

"Why the fuck would you bring us back through here?" the Irishman asked.

"You guys have already been through here?" Garret asked.

"When everything went to shit."

"What happened?"

"We pissed people off."

"People?" Garret asked.

The Irishman looked to the ground and shook his head, like he lost a fight before the first punch. That worried Garret. Even when they rescued the Irishman from Crawford's torture chamber, beat to shit and missing an eye, he maintained a semblance of hope. Now he looked broken, like a glass bottle dropped on concrete.

"What's the plan?" Cody asked.

"That's what we're working on," Garret said. "Maps want to shed some background on what you got us into?"

Maps sighed and said, "Figured we could drive through here, since we had guns and ammo. I wasn't expecting us to lose everything."

"What are you talking about?"

"What kind do you think, Garret? Jesus, man." The Irishman put a hand in front of his face, blocking out the sun.

"You're both being vague. Just tell me what the hell happened."

"Celina is a small town, right? Low population. Hordes of the dead or raiders decimated almost every small town we passed through. Not Celina though. You'd have better luck finding a leprechaun walking down the street than a corpse. All thanks to a biker gang that goes by the name, The

Brotherhood. Of course me and Maps were fortunate enough to run into them. They tried to tax us. And -- well, we don't pay taxes. Especially not to anyone that eats better than us."

"So what? That was months ago. They could have moved on. It will take longer, but we don't have to cut through town. Feels like the right move is to play it safe and go around using the woods as cover, like usual."

The Irishman shook his head. "Bear traps, pitfalls, and worse, wait for us in those woods. They set it up so people have to funnel through town, and BAM -- they take half your shit."

"You think they still hold the town?" Garret asked.

"They seemed pretty keen on community, their leader especially. The bastard acted like he was Robin Hood with his band of merry thieves, thought he was protecting the remnants of his home town or some stupid shit like that. We put a bullet through his head and hightailed it out of there with a squadron of Harley Davidson's on our ass. We never should've come back this way."

Garret pressed his thumbs into his temple, clearly frustrated, and Cody looked disgusted. Janice sat in the shade under a tree, mumbling a prayer. Alyssa massaged her own feet, disinterested in the conversation.

"Why are we here then?" Cody asked.

Garret thought the same thing. Good question Cody. What the hell were they doing here? Garret had trusted Maps as a navigator since he met him. Maps had steered them out of traps, snuck them in broad daylight past bandits, and kept them out of more dangerous situations than Garret cared to remember.

The Irishman stretched his arms. "They killed his mutt."

"Great, we're going to die over a damn dog." Cody hoped the comment cut Maps, but couldn't tell if it even scratched his shell.

"What kind of dog?" Alyssa asked.

"Cody, don't take us through the town. We can take a different route. I saw a road back there," Janice said.

"That road takes you to a highway, the highway will take you to Welrod in seventy miles." The Irishman turned to Maps, "That sound right?"

Maps nodded.

Garret didn't know what to say. If there was another option available, it sure wasn't obvious. They needed rest and water soon. None of them would make it to Welrod. That was clear enough to him. When the words 'seventy miles' came out of the Irishman's mouth, Garret watched the lightbulb above Janice's head blow up. Garret felt the shrapnel from it in her broken gaze.

"Unless everyone is ready to drink their own piss, we move onward. I guess," the Irishman said, with no attempt to hide the annoyance in his voice.

Nobody must have been ready for that. Because they all followed the Irishman's sulking shadow down the hill.

Garret found relief when they weren't immediately surrounded by bikers. Garret had pictured seven motorcycles encompassing the area the moment they stepped into the town. He imagined the bikers wearing black M.C. jackets with white skulls embroidered above the name "Brotherhood". The bikers themselves were skeletons without so much as an ounce of flesh on them, making the skull logo much more appropriate. Thankfully, all he saw on the road was a dinky little town sign with an even dinkier population number.

But after the Irishman's story about Celina, Garret expected at least an ambush by the time they hit main street. Unlike most other places Garret had seen, Celina didn't look that bad. Rotting bodies didn't litter the street, careless drivers hadn't crashed dozens of vehicles through every store front and coffee shop on the block, and no buildings had been burnt to the ground. From what he could see, the place was in good condition.

It reminded him of before, when every day wasn't a struggle to survive. In some ways, this new world made things simpler. No more having to worry about sales pitches, pay raises, and car insurance payments. Looking on the bright side didn't settle his stomach, though.

Together they quickly cut across the street to an alleyway behind a barber shop. The alley provided them with cool shadows, a much needed break from the sun. Garret was ready for another break and knew Maps would want to listen to make sure that they were alone in the district.

"Where did you run into them?" Garret asked.

"A bar, a couple blocks over that way." The Irishman pointed north through the alleyway.

"Of course," Garret said as he stepped into a puddle.

He looked down into the murky water and saw a reflection. He looked lean, not as bony as Maps but still lighter than he had been in years, dirty too, splotches of mud had streaked through his hair, hardened like shit colored gel. Garret picked the clumps of dirt from his hair as he waited for Maps to finish checking the end of the alley. Garret moved up after Maps gave the signal.

Garret peeked around the corner. He noticed a grocery store across the street with a few abandoned vehicles in the parking lot and a smashed open vending machine. Grass had grown rampant across the medians surrounding the store, vines crept up the windows tinted by the darkness inside. Beyond the leaves and vines, Garret could barely make out a case of flavored water on a checkout conveyor belt.

Cody pointed to the store. "Water. Over there."

"Thank you, Jesus," Janice said and bowed her head, mumbling a quick prayer.

"This doesn't look right," Garret said.

"What's wrong?" Alyssa asked.

"What else can you see?" Garret asked.

"Nothing, it's too dark."

Garret shook his head with a sour look on his face. "Someone placed that water there to be seen."

"You're not as stupid as you used to be." The Irishman flashed a grin for a second, then remembered how badly he wanted a drink of water or liquor.

Garret knew the plan. It didn't need to be said. Skip the water, cut through town, and find a river once they were in the clear. It was as safe and solid as a plan needed to be, and best of all, it made total sense. Despite the plan, Cody stared at the water through the dirty store window. Garret grabbed his shoulder. "We will find water once we're out of this town."

Cody didn't listen. He turned around and saw his mother panting like a dying dog. She was pale and her breaths came in uneasy bursts.

"Mom, are you okay?"

"Just catching my breath," she said, but she had been trying to catch her breath for the past ten minutes with no luck.

"What if it was a trap a while ago and now it's not? Whoever put it there could have forgotten about it, or moved on by now. Look around guys, this place is a ghost town.Maps, did you see anything?"

Maps shook his head.

"There could be food in there too and we are just going to pass it up?"

"Is it still a trap?" Alyssa asked.

"Look at mom," Cody said.

"I'm fine," Janice said. She stood up from the pavement and stumbled forward. Cody caught her.

"Mom, you're dehydrated, you need to sit back down." Cody turned to Garret. "You think she can make it another mile in this heat?"

Garret honestly didn't know. He didn't have a doctorate in medicine. They were all dehydrated, exhausted, and sore from a sleepless night of hiking, but none of them had passed out yet and it hadn't even been over twenty-four hours since their last meal.

Cody walked out of the alley only for the Irishman to grab him by his collar and shove him hard up against the brick wall. "Think we came this far by falling into every obvious trap we passed on the way? Get a fucking clue, kid, before you get your family killed."

"Like you give a shit." Cody pushed the Irishman off him. "Asshole." Cody headed out of the alley and out onto the street. "Alyssa, stay with mom. Garret, if anything happens, protect my family."

Garret wanted to chase after him, but didn't. He watched as Cody crossed the street, checking the rooftops above for any spotters.

Cody ducked in front of the cars in the parking lot, like they provided an actual cover. If anyone was watching the front of the store, they would have seen Cody despite his mission impossible style antics. Garret thought about running after him.

Cody forced the sliding door open, walked inside the store, and disappeared behind the dirty glass, only re-appearing for a moment to lift the water off the conveyor belt. Then he disappeared behind the glass again.

Janice closed her eyes and prayed. Her daughter sat at her side. Alyssa bit on her nails and tapped her foot, anxiously waiting for her brother's return.

Cody walked out of the front of the store with his hands on the back of his head. Behind him followed a man wearing coke-bottle glasses. He held a pistol; the barrel pointed at the back of Cody's head. The man spoke into a radio as he waved the barrel of the gun, urging Cody forward.

"Well, shit," Garret said. He made eye contact with Cody, who tried to look brave by keeping a stern face, but Garret could see the poor kid shaking all the way from the alley.

Garret wished Maps had his rifle. The sniper would have already shot the glasses off the man's face. But they didn't have any weapons besides Map's knife, and for the first time since Garret met up with Maps and the Irishman, he felt helpless.

Alyssa jumped up and tried to dash to her brother, but the Irishman swept her up and covered her mouth. She bit down hard on his hand, but the Irishman gripped her tight. "Bite me again, I'll snap your neck."

Janice opened her eyes, then closed them immediately and went back to prayer. Tears rolled down her cheeks. "God please," she said.

Sounds of an engine hummed loudly. An ambulance tore down the street, tires screeching. The emergency vehicle whipped by a concrete median, nearly hitting it, before it turned into the parking lot. It sped through the parking lot toward Cody and the gunman. The driver slammed on the brakes, causing the ambulance to come to an abrupt stop. The vehicle's grill was only a foot from Cody's chest. Even the gunman behind him had jumped out of the way in anticipation of a collision. The driver had a plump, freshly shaved face, except for a weird goatee that corkscrewed down toward the ground. He took off his sunglasses, folded them and hung them on his t-shirt.

"You could have easily flipped the ambulance," the gunman said.

"Least I have some balls, you drive like there's still speed limits."

"Shut up, Tim."

Tim moved slowly out of the vehicle and circled around the back.He opened the door, extended the ramp, and pulled a stretcher out of the back like it was a chore.

The gunman pushed Cody toward the stretcher. "Get on it and lay down."

"Go to hell," Cody said.

The gunman cocked back the hammer on his revolver and lowered the barrel, aiming at Cody's legs. "Make me ask again and I'll knee cap you."

Cody walked toward the stretcher, hands still in the air. He hopped on the stretcher and lay down, his face flush with anger. Tim patted Cody down and then strapped him onto the stretcher. The leather straps tightened around his legs. Cody felt the straps cut the circulation from his legs. He looked toward the alley, praying for a miracle.

To Garret it looked like Cody was an arm's length away, but they might as well have been miles apart. Garret felt sick to his stomach from standing still, watching, and doing absolutely nothing to help. "There's only two of them," he said. Why weren't they helping?

"They could have more men nearby," the Irishman said, Alyssa still tight in his grip. Blood dripped down the hand that covered her mouth.

"Bullshit," Garret said. Cody was right. The Irishman didn't give a shit about what happened to him or his family. "I'll distract them while Maps gets the flank. They only have one gun and I'm tired of watching the people around me die."

"You want to see your wife again?" the Irishman asked.

"I want her to recognize me when she sees me."

Garret ran out of the shaded alley and into the sun-drenched street. Garret didn't care how mad the Irishman would be. If he died, so would their tickets to sipping margaritas in his air-conditioned bunker in Pennsylvania.

"Behind you Four Eyes," Tim said.

Four Eyes turned around and spotted Garret, who trudged up the street towards them. Four Eyes jammed the pistol out in the air, aimed at Garret's chest.

"Trust me, you don't want to make that much noise," Garret said.

"Stop."

"Okay, no problem." Garret stopped twenty yards away and said, "Let my friend go."

"How many more friends you got?"

"Just him." Garret pointed to Cody on the stretcher.

"You should've stayed hidden, dumbass." Four Eyes turned around. "Tim, go over and pat this idiot down."

"Hold on a second." Tim was busy rolling the stretcher up the ramp and into the back of the ambulance. A task made harder by Cody, who struggled against the leather straps, forcing Tim to put his back into it.

"Who the hell are you people?" Garret asked.

"Survivors," Four Eyes said.

"I get it. That's what you tell yourselves to justify whatever awful shit you've done and the bad things you're going to do. You're not a survivor." Garret walked towards him. "You're weak."

"I'll shoot if you take another step."

Garret ignored the threat and continued down the sidewalk toward them.

"Shoot me, and the horde we just lost will be back on track. Bet you don't have enough bullets for them."

Each step Garret took forward, Four Eyes matched him with a step backward.

"Jesus Tim, get over here."

"Fuck, I said one second." Tim shoved the stretcher into the ambulance and slammed the back doors closed. He turned to Garret, unhooked his sunglasses from his shirt, and put them on. "He wants to do it the hard way. No big deal." Tim pulled down on his corkscrew goatee like a train conductor sounding a horn before taking off.

Garret turned around and ran.

"Get him!" Four Eyes yelled.

Garret's feet slapped the sidewalk in a fury as he ran south, back the way he came. He passed the now empty alley and made a right onto Jackson Avenue. Garret picked up the pace when he heard Tim round the corner with a loud, angry huff. He dashed down the street with a hope that Maps would be lurking around the corner with his knife. Instead, he tripped over a crack in the sidewalk, scraping his hands and knees as he hit the concrete. He pushed off the ground, leaving skin and blood behind as he attempted to regain his lead.

He cut down an alley, slid over the hood of a car and ran across the street. The air felt cool, numbing the sting of his fresh scrapes as he breezed around a corner and down another street.

Finally, he checked over his shoulder and sure enough, the heavy set goatee man had gained ground on him. Garret went into overdrive, running faster than he did during his track days. He ran until his heart rode high in his throat. No way he could keep this pace much longer.

Garret stopped in front of the county library and slid past the broken glass door into the single story building. He jogged past the metal detectors and into total darkness. He hoped Tim hadn't seen him enter the building as he turned into the labyrinth of book shelves and ducked down behind a row of books, eyeing the entrance that provided the only source of light.

Tim opened the front door and light poured in behind him. His breath was heavy, sweat drenched his t-shirt like he had jumped into a pool. He leaned against the metal detector as if it were a cane. "OK. That was great fun." He wheezed. "Come on, man, this library ain't that big." Tim surveyed the columns of books and walked slowly, noticing the sunlight fading with each step.

Garret stifled his breath from making too much noise. The taste of stomach acid burned his mouth. He worried his heartbeat was too loud.

Tim kicked over a bookshelf, causing a domino effect of shelves smashing together and books thudding to the ground.

"Nothing behind door number one."

A fragile hand emerged from the sea of books, followed by a cry.

"Found you." Tim pulled a flip knife from his pocket. He climbed over the shelves and books, stepped on the hand till he heard a crack and another cry.

Garret watched from the other side of the library. With his eyes adjusted to the darkness, he could see the fat silhouetted figure atop a mountain of books, stabbing into the ground. Eyes opened along the wall, witnesses to the stabbing. Garret grabbed a hardback dictionary and jogged toward the exit. Howls of the dead bounced around the walls behind Garret as he ran past the metal detectors and toward the front door.

Tim dropped the knife and ran, fear painted on his face. He scrambled toward the exit behind Garret, grazed through the metal detector, and rounded the corner into a flying dictionary. The hardback book crashed into his face and in a marvelous display of poor balance he toppled to the ground, knocking the air from his lungs. The blow rendered him stuck like a beached whale.

Garret hugged the brick wall outside the library. The rev of motors sounded like gunshots over the hollowed, screaming coming from inside the building behind him. Garret ran back the way he came, across the street and back into the alley. In his peripheral vision, a blurred neon green figure flew past the entrance of the alley.

Garret reached the end of the alley and looked both ways for any sign of his friends.All he saw was a person wearing a neon green racing suit perched on a matching neon green ATV.When the rider looked toward him, Garret saw his scratched helmet and a long sheathe slung over his back.

Garret didn't wait for the chase to start. He doubled back into the alley and listened to the ATV charge down the street after him. He stopped underneath a fire escape and considered the possibility of a rooftop pursuit, with him jumping from building to building to escape, but realized such a course of action would simply lead to a pair of broken legs.

A garbage bin sat behind him. Garret lifted the lid exposing a foul smell of trash soup and decided that wasn't a much better move, and closed the lid. Fire escape it is. He rushed up the stairs to a window and tugged at it with his fingers, to no avail.

The rider parked the ATV underneath the fire escape and hopped off. He unsheathed a long, narrow sword. Sunlight shimmered off the blade, motivating Garret to kick out the window. Shards of glass rained down on the green rider as he strolled up the fire escape with the katana in both hands.

Jagged edges of broken glass pricked Garret's shoulder as he climbed into the building. He was in a messy bedroom with piles of clothes spread on the floor, a few paperbacks on a nightstand, and a computer monitor on a desk in the corner.

Garret searched for a weapon but couldn't find anything he could combat a sword with. He lugged the mattress off the bed and shoved it over the open window. A blade pierced through the center of the fabric, nearly sticking Garret in the stomach. He dropped the mattress and ran out of the room, jogging down the hall. Glass crunched in the bedroom behind him as he hustled down the stairs and out through the front door.

Sweat stung his eyes, and his heart thumped with adrenaline. Disoriented, with no time to think, he was no longer aware of what street he was on or which way he was running. It didn't matter. He dashed forward. Garret focused on the rhythm of his feet, carrying him across the pavement, down the street. He passed a bank and the town hall with a dry fountain out front.

A thunderous gunshot cracked a few blocks away. Garret turned around and found a moment's relief that he may have lost his pursuer. He spat as the taste of stomach acid shot up his throat. A wave of light-headedness crashed over him as he climbed into the fountain and lay down on a bed of pennies.

He controlled his breathing and listened to the sound of the summer's breeze overhead. Soon he heard the ATV drive past him without stopping to spoil his hiding spot. Garret lay on his back, looking into the clouds as he plotted his next move.

28

Garret stayed in the fountain for over an hour as if he were part of the cement structure. Sunburned, blistered, and bleeding from both fresh and old wounds. The past three days had felt like months. He graced his sutured gunshot wound with a light touch and brought a bloody finger to his eye. Garret peeked over the edge of the fountain. As far as he could tell, the coast was clear.

The sounds of motors and gunshots were long gone. He had yet to fathom what happened, who got shot, and where everyone was. For the first time in two months, he was alone.

Garret stood up out of the fountain and observed his surroundings. The small town had an abundance of brick buildings that provided the sidewalks with shade. Neatly organized hedge maple trees lined up and down the streets. The cozy, small town style made Garret think of home. Celina had a similar layout to his own hometown, but the charming storefronts felt like a mask trying to cover a sinister face.

He circled back to the grocery store in a way that would've made Maps proud. He wormed his way through overgrown bushes. Thorns pricked his shoulders and back. Compared to the rest of his wounds, the thorns were nothing more than a primitive back scratcher. He worried more than usual.

The ambulance was gone, as were his companions. Garret sighed. He checked the alley and found it empty.

Alone, again.

After a quarter-mile walk down the road, Garret checked multiple alleys, looking for any sign of Maps, the Irishman, or anybody. The sun waned. It would be dark in an hour or two, and nothing scared Garret more than being alone in the dark, surrounded by the dead.

He had a feeling the library wasn't the only place the dead were taking refuge. Despite how tidy the town looked during the day, he had a feeling it wouldn't remain so at night. Garret spent another twenty minutes scouring through various alleyways and nooks, with no luck. At least the psycho swordsman on his ATV was no longer in pursuit.

He made his way through another alley off of the main street. He decided this was the last one before he gave up his search. As he exited the rear of the alley, he stepped onto the back patio of a bar and grill.

The overgrown shrubbery had reclaimed the sides of the building and even the bar's logo. Garret bent down and pulled a loose brick from the side of the building. Not the most glorious weapon, but it would prove effective enough if it came down to it. Though Garret hoped he wouldn't get that close to a ravenous corpse soon. He looked up the side of the building to see if there was anything he could use to climb atop. Last thing he wanted to do was sit awake all night hoping a zombie wouldn't take a bite out of his sleepy face.

The back door to the bar and grill swung open and the barrel of a shotgun extended out, pointed at Garret's chest. "Move and I'll blow your guts out."

Garret's body froze. He dropped the brick and raised his hands above his head. "Please don't shoot. I've already been shot once this week." Garret pointed to his wound. He turned his head over his shoulder to get a look at the man with the gun.

"Keep staring at that wall son."

Garret let out a sigh and continued to stare deep into the red of the bricks.

"You got any weapons?"

Garret shook his head. "I just dropped it. Are you going to make me stare at this wall all night?"

"Maybe."

To Garret, it didn't sound like this man was the raping and murdering type. If he was, chances were his blood would have already painted the bricks.

"I'm just looking for my friends. We got split up. Some guy on an ATV and people in an ambulance were chasing us."

Garret must have said the password, because the barrel of the shotgun was no longer pointed at his spine. A gray old man revealed himself from behind the shadows. The old man had a long salt and pepper colored beard, though it was mostly salt at this point. Garret turned around to face him, hands still in the air.

"Can I put my hands down now?"

The old man either didn't hear the question or ignored him. He just crept down the three back stairs and circled behind Garret.

"Go on." The old man said, his gun still leveled at Garret.

Garret nodded and walked up the back steps and into the bar and grill. The inside was dark besides the few stray rays of light that peeked through the boarded-up windows. The dining area was almost completely vacant. Most of the chairs and tables had been used to barricade the front door and the plethora of windows encircling the establishment.

Garret took it upon himself to take a seat at the bar on one of the few remaining stools. The old man followed him inside, shut the back door and laid a 2x4 across the side. If Maps or the Irishman had been there, they could have taken that opportunity to disarm the old man, but Garret worried that type of maneuver would leave him with a gut full of buckshot.

"My name's Garret. Me and my friends were just trying to pass through. I'm trying to get home to my wife."

The old man couldn't help but laugh. "How long have you been trying to get home, son?"

Good question. Garret had lost count a while ago. "I guess three months, give or take."

"What makes you think you still got a home? My home's gone, and I didn't spend months away from it."

Garret saw the pain on the old man's face. He lost someone, just like everybody else.

"I've just got a feeling."

"Feelings don't mean shit today, son. You don't seem that worried that I've got a shotgun trained on you."

"You don't seem like the killing type," Garret said.

"You'd be wrong." Regret lingered in his voice.

Garret took a deep breath. In case it was his last. But it wasn't. A minute of silence passed and the old man lowered the barrel of his shotgun, but still held it with both hands.

"You said an ambulance was chasing you?"

"Well, an ambulance was there. I think they got one of my friends, Cody. And then the ATV was the one chasing me."

"You're lucky you got away and even luckier you found me before dark."

"So I take it you're not going to blow my guts out?"

The old man grinned, "Name's Charlie."

Charlie extended his hand, and Garret grabbed it. For being an old man, he still had a hell of a grip. Garret felt a moment of happiness, but it quickly slipped away. He remembered his predicament. His friends missing, possibly kidnapped, and there was a good possibility that they were already dead.

"Do you know anything about those guys that were chasing me?"

Charlie's face turned sour. He shook his head and said, "Hate to tell you this, Garret, but your friends are dead. When that ambulance and fleet of ATVs showed up, people started going missing."

Garret felt a chill dash down his spine and sickness spread through his stomach. "Is it The Brotherhood?"

"Where'd you hear about that?"

"Heard there was a biker gang that ran Celina."

"Used to run Celina, they're dissolved now. Their leader took a bullet to the face, and they crumbled after that. They protected many people in this town. More of a militia really, than a gang."

"So who's got my friends?"

"The people on top of the hill. And let me tell you, son, it's not worth going up there to get yourself killed."

Garret slapped both his hands on the bar. "I can't sit here bullshitting while my friends could be dying."

Garret couldn't abandon them. Not after everything they'd been through. Besides, he wouldn't make it another six hundred miles without them. Even if he died, it would be better than sitting on his hands, doing nothing.

Charlie poured Garret some water into a dirty mug. Not that Garret cared about the cleanliness of the cup. At this point he would've drunk water from a dirty toilet. He brought the mug to his lips and drained the glass in one glug. Garret laughed. It tasted so good, unlike any beverage he had before.

"Thanks Charlie, I appreciate it, really. I'm thankful for this water and that you didn't blow me away on that back patio. But, am I free to leave?"

"What if I say no?" Charlie asked.

"Then you'll be spending the night cleaning my blood off this bar."

Garret let his words sink in. He knew Charlie wouldn't shoot him in cold blood.

"Don't expect my old ass to come save you. It's a three-mile walk from here and I'm sure you'll see the smoke from their bonfire. Follow Main Street and make a left up Grove Street."

"Thanks," Garret said as he stood up and made his way to the back door. Before he could lift the 2x4 blocking the door, Charlie tapped his shoulder. Garret whipped around, and Charlie handed him a small revolver.

"It's only got four shots and I recommend you save a bullet for yourself."

"Uh, thanks I guess," Garret said.

"Oh, and if they torture you, don't sell me up the goddamn river, son."

"Sure Charlie, no problem." Garret stepped down onto the overgrown patio, second guessing this courageous act. Charlie's words weren't exactly words of encouragement. Garret couldn't blame him. This was stupid. He wasn't even sure he could shoot a gun and hit a target more than a few yards out, and he was even less sure he could shoot himself if it came down to it.

He shook the thoughts of self-doubt from his head and looked to the sky. A trail of smoke billowed in the air above the hilltop three miles outside of town. Garret tucked the revolver in the back of his waistband and put his blistered feet back to the pavement.

29

THE AMBULANCE CAME to a screeching stop. A smell of burnt rubber collided with the scent of cool air ushered in by the fading sun. The Irishman threw the vehicle in park and looked into the rear-view mirror to see the upset look on his passengers faces, but nobody seemed shocked.

Maps had grown accustomed to the Irishman's crazy driving style, while Cody and Alyssa were busy tending to Janice. She looked even more feeble sitting in the back of the ambulance, and it was clear she could have really used an actual EMT.

Four Eyes was bound to the same stretcher Cody had been strapped to five minutes earlier. Maps and The Irishman had taken full advantage of Garret's distraction and disarmed the ill-trained man. Four Eyes was trying to say something, but only muffled sounds came from beyond the gauze gag in his mouth. Maps stood over him, knife in hand.

"Find any drugs?" the Irishman asked.

"No medicine or anything useful, besides that sparkling water," Cody said. His eyes never left his feeble mother, who quietly sipped her beverage.

Four Eyes squirmed against the leather straps. Maps put an end to that with a wave of his knife, as if he were wagging his finger in a disapproving manner.

The Irishman hopped out of the driver's seat and ducked into the back.

He stood over Four Eyes and shot a glance over to Cody. "Take the girls outside for this."

Alyssa gave the Irishman a mean glare, "I'm not a little girl."

"We're fine here," Cody said.

"Suit yourself." The Irishman ripped the gauze from Four Eyes' throat. Four Eyes responded with a desperate choking sound and a mumble of curses.

"You're all dead," Four Eyes said and then gasped for air.

The Irishman slapped Four Eyes hard across the head. "Speak when spoken to."

"Eat shit."

This time the Irishman grabbed Four Eyes' short hair and whipped the back of his head down against the stretcher with enough force to give him a migraine for a week. He took a moment to give the man another chance to talk back. Silence hung in the air. Four Eyes finally understood the Irishman's set of rules.

The Irishman held up the green walkie talkie for Four Eyes to see and asked, "Who is on the other end of this?"

"Home," Four Eyes said.

"Is that where your acquaintances took my good buddy Garret? Huh? The guy on the ATV or the ugly fuck with the bad facial hair?"

Four Eyes smirked and said, "Your friend is barbecue by now," and spit on the Irishman's face.

The Irishman ignored the saliva as it ran down the side of his cheek. "There's two things I hate in this world, sobriety and cannibals." And with that remark, the Irishman pulled the .38 from his waistband and smashed the butt of the gun down into Four Eyes' face again and again.

As a stream of blood ran down the poor bloke's face, the Irishman cleaned the butt of the pistol off on the captive's shirt. "How many men do you have?"

"One hundred," Four Eyes said and snorted a spray of blood down across his chin.

The Irishman shoved the gauze back into his mouth and patted Four Eyes' bruised cheek. He reached an open hand out towards Maps. "Can I see that knife?"

Maps handed it over without a second thought. The Irishman nodded a thank you and plunged the blade into the side of Four Eyes' stomach. Four Eyes squealed. Muffled screams of pain tried to escape past the gauze.

"Whoops, I think I hit an intestine. That's got to hurt, but luckily I don't think I nicked an artery. So the good news is you've got at least half an hour before you bleed out." The Irishman pulled the knife out and handed it back to Maps casually, as if he had just used it to open a bag of chips.

"I would like to thank you for the information. You've been quite helpful, but I think we're at capacity now."

Maps swung open the back door of the ambulance. A breeze of cool air swept away the scent of fresh iron.

"Thanks again and if you find a surgeon out there, I'm sure she'll be able to save your life." The Irishman concluded his speech and gave the stretcher a hard kick, sending it bouncing out of the ambulance. It careened down the road a good five yards before it toppled over.

Maps swung the back door to the ambulance closed as Janice puked across the floor.

"Ah, shit. Cody, I told you not to let her drink too much water too fast." The Irishman shook his head in disapproval.

"I don't think it was the water," Cody said.

Once Janice finished emptying the rest of her stomach acid onto the floor of the ambulance, she shivered. Cody reached out his arm and grabbed her shoulder. "Come on mom, you're okay."

The Irishman got back into the driver's seat and gave a quick honk on the horn. "We don't have time for this."

"He's the devil," she whispered to her son.

The Irishman shoved his foot on the gas. He never needed to ask Four Eyes for directions. The smoke in the sky might as well have been a GPS. In less than a minute they had covered a mile, thanks to the Irishman's philosophy on driving.

He abruptly slowed down as they reached the top of the hill. He hooked the wheel to the left and turned the ambulance down a long private driveway. The Irishman pumped the brakes, stopping the vehicle before they were out from under the cover of the trees. The driveway curved up ahead where the foliage thinned.

"We're close enough. Wouldn't want to ruin the surprise," the Irishman said as he threw the vehicle into park.

Maps opened the back door with care and slid out onto the pavement. He tucked his bloody knife into the sheath that hung from his belt. The Irishman inspected his newfound revolver, opened the chamber and gave it a spin, noting the five rounds. He slapped it closed and put it in his front pocket before climbing out of the ambulance.

"Do me a favor and monitor your bat shit, mom, okay?"

Cody ignored the comment and followed them out of the ambulance. "Alyssa, take care of mom, we'll be back soon."

"Cody, be safe."

"Yeah sis, will do."

Cody closed the back door as quietly as possible and hurried to catch up behind the Irishman and Maps, who were already turning up the bend in the driveway.

"You sure this is even the right place?"

"You smell that? Fire's got to be out back," the Irishman said.

They followed the driveway another hundred feet before they reached an iron gate connected to two high brick posts. There was a small, black kiosk with a keypad. The gate must have been eight feet tall, but it only took Maps a handful of seconds to climb up and over it.

The Irishman let out a sigh of disappointment as he struggled to scale up the black iron gate.

"Give me a boost, won't you?"

Cody interlocked his hands together, giving The Irishman some much needed help. The Irishman landed on the other side. Cody scaled the gate almost as smoothly as Maps had.

"Hey, you're not as useless as you look," the Irishman laughed.

The driveway continued for another few hundred feet, leading up to a massive four-car garage attached to a mansion. The mansion itself seemed to stretch forever. If they had to search room by room, by the time they found Garret, he'd be human jerky.

The mansion rested atop of the hill with an extravagant lawn that extended down a huge slope. It was the type of yard that would require an entire lawn care maintenance squad to keep in tip-top condition. Thankfully, it had been months since its last treatment and the grass was almost two feet tall, giving more than enough cover for Maps, the Irishman, and Cody to get a closer look.

They lay on the front lawn, listening to the distant sounds of conversation and wood crackling on the fire in the backyard.

Maps led the way, crawling up the side of the lawn until they reached its peak. There wasn't a soul to be seen in the front, but there were people inside the house and out in the backyard. The house was nearly fully lit, grandiose windows with meticulous designs allowed the light to escape from inside.

A few minutes later, Maps went on the move. Silently, the Irishman followed him, with Cody close behind. They crept up to the side of the mansion, keeping their bodies clear of the windows. With his back to the brick wall of the building, Maps inched to the side of the massive window and peered into the living area. He spotted nothing of significance other than thousands of dollars worth of lavish furniture. They continued across the front of the house, ducking underneath windows until they reached the side of the building.

Wood crackled in the backyard and a conversation grew louder as they neared the back of the mansion. Maps peeked his head out to get a look at the enormous backyard and patio. Two men stood out on the patio in front of a smoker and two big grills, the type of grills that have three racks with enough room to barbeque for the entire neighborhood. The grill master was turning meat with a pair of metal tongs and brushing it with sauce.

Maps ducked back to the side of the house. There was a locked door that led to the garage, but Maps lacked the tools to get inside. They could have easily kicked the door in at the cost of their element of surprise.

"What are we waiting for?" Cody asked.

"He's trying to get a count on how many are inside," the Irishman said.

"I count two," Cody said.

"They got a grill full of meat and those two don't look like fat fucks. There's at least five."

"They could be gutting Garret right now," Cody said.

"Shut up."

They heard the patio door slide open. Multiple voices escaped from inside the house.

"Did Craig and Troy check back in yet?" somebody asked the grill master.

"No, but they're always late to check-in. Come on, let's eat. Dinner's served."

30

GARRET JOGGED over a mile before slowing down to a brisk walk. If he ran the entire way, he would pass out before he even got to his destination. The sun set and nightfall swept over Celina. Garret didn't want to be outside much longer. He smelled the dead nearby, but he'd seen none. Every few minutes he stopped to turn around and make sure he wasn't being followed. The road curved and he came to a stop. There was an object on the side of the road, turned over. Garret jogged up to it. It was the stretcher Cody had been strapped to.

"Cody, you there?" Garret stood over the object and winced. It was completely blood soaked. Torn pieces of a body beside it. Garret's eyes welled up with tears. "I'm so sorry."

Thoughts raced through his mind. He should have been able to save him, but he didn't. No, he was still too damned weak to protect his friends. What an outstanding leader I am, he thought to himself. Garret kicked the stretcher hard with his foot.

"Sorry, Cody."

Garret continued down the road. Tears streamed down his face as he put every ounce of energy he had into running. The cool night air broke against his cheeks, drying his tears.

"I'll kill every one of those bastards. I swear to God." Garret spoke to himself, his heart in his throat. What if everyone was already dead? He imagined discovering the bodies of Maps, Janice, Alyssa and the Irishman. What more could he have done to save them?

Garret finally stopped to catch his breath. A harsh sting radiated through his lungs, his heart still racing. If everyone was already dead, he would just be walking into the grinder. Like he stood a chance against the people atop the hill, if Maps and the Irishman couldn't even survive. He hawked mucus to the ground and cleared his head of those worthless thoughts. They weren't dead, they couldn't be. Not yet, anyway.

He heard twigs cracking, the brush rustling behind him.

Garret looked to his left and stared into the woods. Two corpses meandered toward the road. Garret pulled the pistol from his waistband and they stopped. Garret's eyes met with theirs. Cold gray and lifeless. They didn't move. Instead, they just watched him. What the hell were they doing?

"Are you afraid of me?" Garret called out to the corpses.

The two zombies remained as still as the trees they were standing by. Garret waved the pistol in the air. Slowly they stepped backwards into the woods, one step at a time.

Garret didn't have time to be disturbed. He tucked the gun back into his waistband and continued up the road.

An open shed stood tall, twenty yards south of the patio. Thanks to the small light affixed to the middle of it, Maps could make out four ATVs inside. With confidence he crossed out from the side of the mansion, leaving the Irishman and Cody waiting, and snuck across the backyard like a ghost. A few yards to the side of the shed stood a deer field dressing post. No deer were strung up, but he could smell blood.

He put his ear to the side of the shed and listened. After a minute that felt like an eternity, he was certain nobody was inside.

Maps walked through the open door. Inside were three chest freezers and two big sinks. He stuck two fingers into the drain and pulled up a tiny piece of flesh. He flicked the pink slimy piece back into the sink and walked over to the freezers. Inside he found dozens of vacuumed packed bags of meat. Maps shut the lid and inspected the other two freezers, only to find much of the same.

The entire shed was stocked like a meat processing plant. They even had meat grinders, two dehydrators, and a station set up to vacuum pack their kills. Maps glossed over the four ATVs sitting there, noticing the keys were all still inside the ignition. Not a bad plan B if everything went to shit. Maps grabbed a fillet knife off the counter next to the sinks and ducked out of the shed.

The Irishman sat on the side of the mansion, rolling his head and stretching his neck. Cody stood next to him, tapping his foot as quietly as possible. His nervousness coursed through his legs.

"Relax," the Irishman said.

"How are you so calm? That guy said there were 100 cannibals in there."

"He was bullshitting us," the Irishman said. "And if you didn't notice, we waltzed right in here. I've robbed meth heads with better security measures in place."

Cody digested that information, but it didn't make him feel any better. As he was thinking about what kind of person the Irishman was before the end of the world, Maps popped back around the corner. The man was so quiet neither Cody nor the Irishman had heard him coming.

Maps handed the fillet knife over to Cody, who accepted it reluctantly. Cody thought back to The Irishman sticking Four Eyes in the gut with Maps's knife and shuddered. He would never do something like that.

"Garret's not here," Maps whispered.

"What makes you say that?" the Irishman asked.

"They would already be field dressing him."

"How do you know he's not inside?" Cody said.

"He doesn't," the Irishman answered.

"We'd be better off going back into town to look for him."

"The poor bastard might be locked up in their cellar for all we know," the Irishman said.

They heard the patio door slide open again. Laughter roared out from inside the mansion. It sounded like a party. The grill master's voice carried out into the backyard. "I told you to lock the shed. I can see the damn door open from here."

A teenager shot out into the backyard, barreling towards the shed's open door. A Katana swayed on his back. Once he got to the shed, he slammed the door shut in a hurry, retrieved a key from his pocket, and locked the door. He rushed back toward the mansion, but just as he reached the back patio, the Irishman popped out from the side of the house and pulled the kid into a headlock with the barrel of his .38 kissing the side of his head.

"Go ahead, slowly. Let's go inside and meet the family. Yell or say a word and I'll snap your neck like a twig."

The teenager couldn't say a word if he had wanted to. In fact, he could barely breathe with the death grip the Irishman had around his throat. The Irishman shoved him forward, up the two back steps and inside the mansion, through the open patio door.

Cody and Maps followed a few feet behind. The Irishman walked the kid through the lavish kitchen that boasted a gorgeous island, a double oven, refrigerator and expensive marble counters. The voices got louder as they moved through the kitchen toward the dining room.

A giant dinner table stretched from one end of the dining room to the other. About a dozen people sat at the table, laughing, drinking, and feasting. There were plates with tons of food, bottles of wine, and even freshly baked bread.

The Grill Master sat at the head of the table, drinking from a large glass. A bloody plate of meat sat in front of him. He smiled to see his son return from outside, only to freeze when he saw the man behind him with a gun to his child's head.

The conversations stopped, and silence gradually captured the room. There were eight men and four women sitting at the table. A group of burly, mean looking bastards sat at the far end across from the Grill Master, their hatred filled gazes focused on the Irishman and his revolver.

"Sorry to interrupt your feast." The Irishman squeezed his hostage's neck.

One of the ugliest, meanest looking guys at the end of the table jumped up out of his seat with a steak knife in his hand.

"Sit the fuck down or I shoot," the Irishman snarled, spit flying out of his mouth and onto the food in the center of the table.

"Do as he says," the Grill Master said.

The ugly man listened and sat down, the knife still gripped tight in his hand, his eyes shooting daggers. The Irishman knew the man wanted to tear into his flesh.

"We have food, vehicles, supplies. What do you want?" the Grill Master asked.

"That bottle of Merlot, give it here," the Irishman said.

Without hesitation, they passed the bottle down. The Irishman released the teenager out of the chokehold, and the kid fell down to his knees, choking for air. The Irishman swept the room with the pistol in his right hand and snatched the bottle with his left.

"Take the goddamn cork out."

The woman popped the cork, and the Irishman took the bottle to his lips and drank.

"Please sit down and join us. You don't have to do anything crazy," the Grill Master said.

The Irishman couldn't respond because he was still working on draining the bottle to its last drop. When he finished, he tossed the bottle to the ground.

"I have a pretty shit palate, but I don't eat fucking people," the Irishman said.

Maps crossed to the other side of the table, hunting knife in hand. He stood behind the Grill Master, ready to put the blade into the base of the cannibal's skull.

"We do what we have to do to survive, to feed my family," the Grill Master said. "We can't just starve."

One of the tough guys at the end of the table spoke up, "That bastard can't shoot us all, he only has six shots."

The Irishman snapped the pistol to him and fired. The slug hit the tough guy straight in the nose and blew out the back of his head onto the expensive dining chair. Screams erupted from the table.

"Stop it," the Grill Master screamed at both the Irishman and the people sitting at the table.

The Irishman spotted another bottle of red wine sitting in front of a woman, hands over her eyes, crying.

"Everyone relax. We're going to be asking a few questions and then we'll be on our way. But first give me that bottle. The woman's crying quieted as she grabbed the half empty bottle of wine and handed it over to the Irishman. The miraculous sensation of alcohol danced on his tongue, trickling down the back of his throat, adding to the pit of fire in his belly.

The Irishman looked down at the meat on the table; it didn't look like beef, pork or chicken. He drained the half empty bottle, tossed it to the side, and swiped a roll from the table.

He spoke with his mouth full of food. "Do you have a feast like this every night?"

The Irishman aimed the question to the south end of the table, where it looked like all the enforcers sat. They must be the armed guard, caught with their pants down. If they had guns on them, they would have already been shooting. Three of the cannibals were especially mean looking. Beefy, tattooed, with untamed facial hair and the eyes of predators in the night. The Irishman made a mental note to shoot them first, with the remaining four rounds in his revolver.

Nobody spoke up, probably a result of the last speaker losing a chunk of his head to a slug. "Let me ask again. Do you eat this good every night?"

The Grill Master looked down at the table and said, "We're just trying to survive, doing the same as you."

The Irishman burst into a loud, sinister laughter that rattled the room. Everyone in the room seemed afraid of him and what he might do, including Cody.

"The same as us?" the Irishman laughed again. He slapped his leg with the side of the gun and spit pieces of dinner roll onto the floor. "I may be a murdering bastard, but I'd be a fucking vegan before a cannibal." The Irishman wiped the food particles from his face and staggered back a step, aiming the barrel at the Grill Master.

The attack dogs at the south end of the table had enough of sitting around. Maps moved to the edge of the room, knife in hand with all his concentration on the enforcers. They gripped steak knives in their hands, just waiting for the right moment to lunge out of their chairs and end the Irishman's drunken rambling.

"How many people is that?" The Irishman pointed his gun at the pile of meat sitting in the center of the table. "Two people? Three people's worth? I'm sorry I just don't know how much meat you can get off a human."

No one answered.

The Irishman kicked the teenager in the back of his knee, causing him to fall back to the ground. The boy's father stood up out of his chair. "Leave now," the Grill Master said.

The Irishman just laughed.

Nerves ran down Maps' spine. He could see the attack dogs shifting uncomfortably in their seats, itching for their master to let go of their leash.

Cody piped up from the corner of the dining room. "Ask about Garret."

The Irishman smiled and swooped the pistol back towards the Grill Master.

"Are you eating our friend, Garret? Light brown hair, skinny guy with a loudmouth."

The teenager on his knees said, "No, he got away."

The Irishman didn't know if it was the alcohol or just the good news, but he couldn't help but plaster a huge grin on his face.

"Where was he?"

"Back in town. I chased him from the library and lost him."

Maps smiled. Garret was alive.

"Good boy," the Irishman said.

"We didn't kill your friend. Please, just leave."

"Let's go," Cody said.

The Irishman chuckled. "Yeah, let's go. Let them gather their guns and shoot us on our way out."

The Irishman nodded. His sought after buzz rose through his body like he was on a cloud and for a few moments he forgot all about the end of the world and everything else that lay in ruin.

He smiled, staggered backwards, and lowered the revolver. "Yeah, let's leave."

A sense of relief filled the room.

"On second thought." He quickly raised his pistol again and fired into the enforcers sitting at the south end of the table.

One bullet struck the biggest guy in the neck, the second bullet went through his head, the third bullet hit his neighbor in the cheek and the fourth bullet ended up in the center of the third man's chest.

The dinner table erupted, a few dove from their chairs to hide underneath. Others made a break for the exit, only to be greeted by Maps, the human meat grinder. The way he moved with his knife was like something out of a nightmare. He slashed the throats of two cannibals trying to get past him. A third man charged directly at him with a steak knife in his hand. Maps greeted the man with six inches of serrated metal in his guts and twisted the knife from his victim's hand.

The Irishman tucked the pistol into his waistband, yanked a steak knife from the table and charged The Grill Master, who stood frozen by his dining chair. The Irishman drove the knife deep into his neck and left it there. Blood spurted from the Grill Master's throat as he fell face forward onto the table.

Screams waned as Maps cut the remaining cannibals down.

Almost everyone sitting at the table was dead on the ground or laying across the table with bullet holes and stab wounds. Only the teenager laying on the ground curled up in the fetal position and a sobbing woman survived. Cody remained standing in the corner, his knife unbloodied.

The Irishman turned to him. "You were some great help. How about you watch these two while we scavenge some supplies?"

Cody didn't respond. The horrors he had just witnessed replayed themselves in his mind again and again.

The Irishman finally stepped over to him and slapped Cody across the face. "Wake up and watch them, okay?"

Cody swallowed and nodded. Maps and the Irishman disappeared from the room, leaving Cody to stare into the mess of corpses and broken people left alive.

31

GARRET REACHED the mansion in a state of total exhaustion. The driveway hit an incline, making each remaining step a battle. His knees hurt. Inflamed tendons and muscles cried for him to stop. But then he spotted the ambulance parked in front of the mansion's iron gate. Why would the ambulance be outside the gate? He quietly approached the vehicle and peered through the back window. Empty.

Garret ducked off to the side of the road, keeping his head on a swivel. He had no intentions of being turned into a late-night snack after this trek. The woods seemed clear, but Garret couldn't see over ten feet in front of him, thanks to the darkness. There was no doubt in his mind that there were monsters lurking nearby.

The gate rattled as Garret scaled the front and made a noisy landing on the other-side. Pain shot up the side of his abdomen. He gritted his teeth and pressed forward. Were his friends already dead? Doubtful. He remembered the quick series of gunshots he'd heard twenty minutes ago.

An engine roared to life, startling Garret. It was the same sound the ATV had made earlier when he was being chased. Except this time there was nowhere to run. Not that he even had the energy to escape. It was about to be over, and there wasn't a damn thing Garret could do to stop it. How stupid, he thought. How could he rescue anyone?

Garret pulled the revolver from his pants and aimed toward the two shining lights. Before he pulled the trigger, a familiar figure appeared atop the ATV. It took Garret a second, but when he realized who he was looking at, he lowered the pistol.

"Ah, Garret, I see you're late to the party as usual," the Irishman cackled.

"There was a guy with a sword chasing me. Is he in there?"

"Maybe amongst the bodies. We crashed their dinner, thinking you were being served up."

Garret nodded. "I thought the same thing was happening to you. Is everyone okay?"

"Oh, everyone's great, everything's great, Garret," the Irishman slurred.

Garret smelled wine and death on his breath. Specks of wet blood covered the Irishman's face, accompanied by a victorious grin. It was the same facial expression the Irishman had after he'd taken Sheriff Crawford into the woods and cut out his eyes. Chills fluttered down Garret's spine as if he were standing in front of the grim reaper himself.

"Are Cody and his family okay?" Garret asked.

"Yeah, they're all inside."

"Nice house, huh?" the Irishman grabbed Garret's shoulder. "Glad you weren't their dinner."

"Me too."

A loud crash from inside the house, disrupted their reunion. Without a word, Garret chased behind the Irishman as he stumbled around the house to the patio and inside through the sliding glass door.

They rushed into the dining room, the scene of a total massacre. The once white table cloth dripped blood to the floor. Bodies lay hunched over their dinner, face down on their plates. A pile of corpses were piled against the edge of the wall, their mouth's agape in terror; almost as if they could see the hell they were going to in their last breaths.

A teenager sat over the corpse of his mother, crying hysterically. Cody stood about six feet from the boy, staring down at the blood on his knife, completely entranced by the blade.

"I didn't mean to," Cody said, his eyes never moving from the gleaming blood on his blade. Garret looked at the fresh scratches on Cody's face.

"She just ran at me. I yelled at her to stop, but..." Cody trailed off, lost in the emotions flooding his brain.

"It's okay, Cody, it's going to be fine. Why don't you give me the knife and go see your family?" Garret asked.

Cody looked up at Garret, unable to make eye contact.

"Yeah, okay," Cody said and handed the knife to Garret before he walked away.

"Bastards, I'm going to kill you all," the teenager screamed.

The Irishman stood over the boy like a giant and smashed his fist into his face, sending him to the ground. The Irishman kicked him in the side, but got no response in return.

"Out cold," the Irishman said without a second glance and went into the kitchen, scavenging through cabinets, looking for more booze.

Garret tried to avert his eyes from the horrifying scene, but when he tried looking at the ground all he saw were blood streaked shoe prints on the hardwood floor. It felt like the walls were closing in around him, despite the dining room being obnoxiously huge, like the rest of the house. Garret walked over to the unconscious teenager and bent down to check his pulse.

"Why are you trying to give a fuck?" the Irishman asked. He grew irritated as each cabinet failed to provide him with another drink.

"You killed his family."

"We killed his family, Garret. You might not have been here in person, but you were sure here in spirit. We killed them for you."

The Irishman slammed a cabinet door shut hard enough to snap it off its hinges. He proceeded onto the next one as he grew more frustrated. "Fuck feeling guilty."

"What?" Garret asked. How did the drunk prick know he felt responsible for every drop of blood that had been shed tonight?

"They don't deserve your guilt, remorse or for their rotting piece of shit bodies to be mourned."

"They were still human," Garret said.

The Irishman burst out laughing as if Garret were a standup comedian, reaching the peak of his routine. The brute abandoned his search of the cabinets and staggered over to the dining room table where he swept a piece of meat that resembled a medium-rare veal cutlet off of a plate and held it in the air.

"This is human," the Irishman said as he squeezed the piece of meat. The red juices dripped onto the tablecloth.

"Looks like beef to me," Garret said.

"You see any cows out back?" the Irishman asked.

Garret shook his head. The sight of the meat went from looking appetizing to making Garret feel nauseous.

"I'm going to find a bathroom," Garret said. He just had to get out of the dining room. The entire room was making him sick. He wandered down a hallway, trying not to look at the pictures of the now slaughtered family that hung from the walls. The guilt was like a stone in the pit of his stomach.

At the end of the hall Garret walked into the bathroom, flipped the light-switch on and made it to the toilet, where he knelt down and vomited the little stomach acid he had left into the immaculate bowl. Garret stood up and walked to the sink. He turned on the faucet and to his surprise, hot water actually spewed out.

Garret washed the dirt and grime from his face. He grabbed a cloth from the sink's cabinet and squirted some hand soap onto it and began washing the dried mud out of his hair. By the time Garret finished, he realized he probably could have taken a shower. What a luxury. He long ago gave up on the hopes of a shower, let alone a hot one. He peeled the bandage back on his wound and winced.

Garret opened the medicine cabinet and pulled out some antibiotic ointment. He carefully cleaned the wound with the cloth and plenty of soap before he patted it dry and administered a healthy dose of antibiotic ointment. It stung for a moment before going back to a numb, fiery pain. He finished dressing his wound with some gauze. His dizzy spell subsided, but the stone in his stomach remained.

When Garret got out of the bathroom, he found everyone gathered in the living room. Janice lay sleeping on the couch, and Cody sat with Alyssa on a sectional sofa.

"Can we stay here?" Alyssa asked Cody as she laid back on the comfortable sofa, barely able to keep her eyes open.

Cody didn't answer, like the words had just flown past him. His face remained blank, despite his sister's shining mood. Of course neither she nor Janice had seen the bloodbath. They must have come through the front of the house, Garret thought to himself. If they had seen the dining room, there would be a completely different tone in this room.

A collection of supplies gathered from the house lay in the center of the room. The pile included cans of food, a half dozen cases of bottled water, a Katana, a twelve-gauge shotgun with a box of shells, a compound bow with ten arrows and a cardboard box full of toiletries and first aid kits scavenged from the first and second floor bathrooms.

Garret took mental notes of the new inventory. As he was counting the water and cans of food, he heard footsteps in the hallway. Maps walked into the living room with a disdainful look on his face. "You should probably see this."

Garret didn't need to ask Maps what happened. The man seemed more like a machine than ever before. His eyes were empty, almost as lifeless as the human husks wading through the woods.

Together they walked down a flight of steps to the basement, finding a lavish display of wealth. Expensive looking paintings lined the walls. They walked past a collection of workout equipment occupying most of the open space, down a dimly lit hall toward what looked like a guest bedroom.

The Irishman stood in the doorway with a stoneface. He extended his arm as if he'd suddenly gained a set of manners, encouraging Garret to go first.

"What's going on?" Garret asked.

"Check this out."

An awful sense of cold despair gripped the room. The guest bedroom looked like it belonged in a slum. The carpet had been pulled up, leaving exposed nails on the dirt covered floor. A single sheetless mattress lay in the back corner. On the mattress lay a naked man covered in dirt and his own waste. His hands were bound behind his back with wire ties so tight they cut into his skin. A dirty plate rested inches from his face.

At first, Garret believed the man to be dead. Until Garret saw his eyes pop open.

"Hey sir, are you okay?" Garret asked. No response.

What a dumb question. The man looked terrible. "Are you okay?" More like "Are you still alive? Did these cannibals cut out your tongue? Can you talk?" That would have been a more appropriate line of questioning.

The man grunted and said, "Water please."

Garret ran upstairs and in a few minutes returned with a small cup of water. He bent down over the man and dribbled some water past his cracked lips, into his mouth.

The man coughed and lay his head back onto the bed. "Where's Cindy?"

"Uh, I'm sorry I don't know who that is," Garret said.

The man groaned. Obviously, that wasn't the answer he had wanted to hear. Garret realized how painful it was for the man to speak.

"Don't bullshit the man, she's dead," the Irishman said.

"We don't know that."

Maps grabbed Garret by the shoulder and just shook his head. A part of Garret knew Maps was right, but didn't want to admit it. The poor guy had been through hell;dehumanized, treated worse than cattle in a slaughter-house, and his wife was most likely vacuum sealed in one of the many bags in the freezer out back.

The man was trying to mouth something, but Garret couldn't make it out.

"Did you check every room in this house?" Garret asked.

"Yes," Maps said.

The man on the mattress met Garret's eyes with his own and said, "Kill me."

"No, you're going to be okay, it's all going to be okay."

The man pointed to the gun tucked away in Garret's waistband and mouthed the words again. Garret turned away from the decrepit man. He couldn't stand to look at him anymore, but he could still feel the man's sorrow spreading up his back.

"Give it here, come on," the Irishman said to Garret. "If you won't put the poor bastard out of his misery, I will."

Garret couldn't say another word, no matter how badly he wanted to argue with the Irishman. As much as Garret wanted to deny the man's request, how could he? Garret pulled the gun from his belt and handed it over to the Irishman.

"Sorry about all this," the Irishman told the broken man as he lay a pillow over his face, pressed the gun into it, and pulled the trigger. The pillow did little to muffle the gunshot, but it stopped any blood from spraying back onto the Irishman's face. He held the pistol out to Garret.

Garret said, "Keep it."

The Irishman stuck the pistol in his pocket and walked out of the disgusting room. Maps gave Garret a pat on the back and followed the Irishman. There were still supplies to organize before they hit the road again.

Garret remained in the room for some time. He wasn't sure if he had been sitting there next to the corpse for minutes or hours. Even though he hadn't known him, he felt the man's pain. Garret felt his anxiety flowing back through his chest. He wondered if Emily was still alive. If she'd seen the same horrors that he had. Garret knew if he gave up hope, then his will to live would be gone, like the man whose body lay beside him.

32

GARRET WOKE up an hour before sunrise thanks to a light slap on the face from the Irishman. The pungent smell of wine on his breath made Garret cringe. He assumed the Irishman spent the rest of the night drinking while he stood watch.

"Are you drunk?" Garret asked as his eyes adjusted to the light.

"They had quite the wine cellar," the Irishman burped and left the room, leaving Garret alone.

Garret didn't even remember falling asleep the previous night. He must have crashed the second he hit the plush king-size mattress in the guest bedroom. The luxurious comfort tempted him to stay in bed, but knew Maps would be eager to get back on the move. They never stayed in one place long, and this would be no exception.

Quiet like this never lasted long. Thoughts of his wife overcame him. They were getting closer, gaining ground. She'd felt so far out of reach for so long. Now he at least could see her shadow, smell her flowery scent.

"Hang in there," he whispered.

Garret eased himself out of the guest bedroom and into the mansion's hallway. As he walked toward the living room, he averted his eyes from the rows of family pictures that hung from the wall. He felt as if their eyes were burning into his back like an out-of-control grease fire. More lives need-lessly wasted.

At the end of the hall, Cody grabbed Garret's arm. His chilly hand jolted Garret awake faster than any espresso could.

"Damn, Cody, you almost scared me into an early grave."

Garret observed the wrinkles on Cody's face. He looked as if he had aged a decade overnight. Heavy bags hung under his eyes. Blood and dirt still covered his face.

"What's wrong Cody? You should take a hot shower while you still can."

"Garret, I want you to come with us."

"What are you talking about?" Garret asked, despite knowing what Cody meant. But he had to get him talking. He needed to hear Cody out, reassure him, and convince him to stay.

"You're not like them, Garret, we're not like them. What I did last night - - I can't become that," Cody said.

"I know they've done bad things and so have I. We might have to do it again, too. This world isn't how it used to be. It forces good people to do bad things."

"There's a difference between killing to survive and killing in cold blood. Garret, they murdered almost a dozen people last night. I killed an unarmed woman."

"They were cannibals," Garret said, hoping that justification would shut Cody down. Garret could see the uneasiness in his eyes, the guilt, sorrow, and confusion.

"How can you know that they all deserved to die? Did you even see the dining room? Go fucking look for yourself, Garret. You're delusional."

Garret ran a hand through his hair, "I already saw it."

There wasn't a doubt in his mind; the dining room was disgusting. The aftermath of a slaughter.

"And you're OK with that?" Cody pointed to the room.

"What would you have done if you thought they had your sister?"

They split the supplies between the ambulance, and the pickup truck parked in the garage. The Irishman and Maps had done a hell of a job scavenging anything of value from the mansion. They packed the bed of the pickup truck tight with boxes of canned food, toiletries, wine and gasoline siphoned from the generator.

Maps had prepared two ATVs to ride in front of the pickup truck. He had argued with the Irishman over whether they should ride three ATVs alongside the truck, but decided it would be best to just siphon the gasoline from the third ATV and use it to get an extra 100 miles out of the truck.

The Irishman had funneled the rest of an open wine bottle into his canteen that he kept strapped around his shoulder. He took one last swig from the bottle and threw it across the garage; it shattered against the concrete floor. Cody ignored the drunk as he shuffled Alyssa and Janice into the truck's cabin.

"Why the long face?" the Irishman asked, practically shouting, not realizing how loud he actually was.

Cody shut the truck's passenger door and crossed the front to the driver's side, not answering the Irishman.

"I got it, you don't like me much," the Irishman spit on the ground. "But don't worry kid, the feeling's mutual."

Cody let out a frustrated sigh and turned to face the drunk. "I'm not a kid. There's a kid in there, the one you tied up and left to lie with the bodies of his parents."

The Irishman smiled. "Don't worry about the boy, we're leaving him with a lifetime supply of food. We'll cut him loose when it's time to leave. Sympathy will get you killed." The brute took a step toward Cody and said, "They'd be bleeding your ass out in that shed if Garret's stupid ass didn't pull you out of their trap."

"Fuck you."

"How'd it feel when you plunged your knife into that woman's chest? You get a hard-on? Nobody told you to fucking kill her. That shit's on you."

Cody charged the Irishman, catching him by surprise. They crashed to the ground. Cody wrestled on top of him and punched the brute hard in his mouth, causing his teeth to rattle. The Irishman retaliated with a jab to the boy's gut. The Irishman shoved him off and rolled to the side. He stood up, touched the stream of blood running down his cheeks, and smiled.

"I hope you can hit harder than that," the Irishman said to Cody as he let him get back on his feet. "Come on, again."

Cody charged forward, but this time the Irishman shifted to the side and Cody crashed into the wall. While he attempted to recover, the Irishman swooped in from behind and put him in a chokehold.

Cody sunk his fingernails into the Irishman's forearm, peeling flesh back as he tried to escape the brute's viselike grip. His vision blurred, consciousness quickly fading away.

"Go to sleep," the Irishman said.

A gunshot rang through the garage. The Irishman let go of Cody and tumbled backwards to the ground. Cody stumbled to his sister, who held her Glock, still aimed at the Irishman. The brute looked down at the gaping hole in his left foot. "Fucking bastard," he spat.

"Give me the gun." Cody ripped the pistol from Alyssa's hands and yelled, "Get in the truck!"

The Irishman edged his hand toward the .38 in his waistband.

"Don't do it."

"One of us dies here."

As the Irishman inched his fingers around the butt of his gun, the door to inside the house swung open, and Garret dashed out.

"Everyone stop it! I don't know what the hell is going on here, but stop." Garret stood between them, in the line of fire.

"Move, they fucking shot me," the Irishman said, the pistol aimed at Garret's back.

Cody spat blood to the ground and screamed, "He almost killed me. Garret, get out of the way!"

Garret raised his hands in the air. "Both of you can shoot through me then. If anybody else dies today, it'll be me."

Silence hung in the air. Garret stood his ground. Eventually, they lowered their weapons.

"Get in the truck and leave," Garret said.

The Irishman struggled to stand, wobbling as he leaned up against the wall. "They're not taking half of our supplies."

Garret walked over to the Irishman and presented his palm. The brute huffed and handed over the pistol while Cody and Alyssa hurried into the front seats of the truck.

"At least get the wine."

Garret sighed. The adrenaline slowly wore off. Damned idiots. He wiped sweat from his brow as he pulled a box of wine and a first-aid kit from the pickup's bed.

The engine roared to life, tires squealing as they peeled out of the garage, picking up enough speed to blast through the front gate. None of them looked back.

33

LESS THAN FIFTY miles north of Celina was where they found them. A trail of run over corpses led to the crash site. Their truck was flipped over on the side of the road.

Garret's heart dropped as he stared out the passenger side window at the destruction.

"Pullover, now."

Maps hit the brakes, bringing the ambulance to a stop. Garret jumped out of the ambulance, rushing to the side of the road.

"Be quick. That horde could still be in the area," the Irishman said.

A few tears rolled down Garret's cheek. He wiped them away as he examined the truck. It looked like they tried to plow through a blockade of the dead, which caused them to veer off the road and flip over. Garret hoped they made it out alive, against all odds. His body trembled with despair.

"Goddamnit." Garret slapped his hand against the vehicle. Cody was missing the lower half of his body. Strips of flesh dangled from his torn face. Neither Alyssa nor Janice were in better shape. It was too much for him to bear. Garret fell to his knees. He reached through the broken window and grabbed Cody's collar, pulling his torso toward him.

"What the fuck are you doing?" the Irishman asked. The brute carefully maneuvered out of the back of the ambulance, keeping his weight on his right foot. "We don't have time for this."

Garret shook his head as he pulled Cody's torso through the window. "We're going to bury them."

"With what? We don't have a shovel or nothing. Let's get the hell out of here before the same thing happens to us."

Cody's eyes popped open and his arms shot forward, wrapping around Garret. His nails tore strips of skin from his back as he sank his teeth into Garret's shoulder. Garret toppled backwards as Cody thrashed against him and whipped his head back with a chunk of flesh clenched between his teeth.

The Irishman dragged Cody off Garret while Maps rushed to his aid and sunk his knife into the top of Cody's skull.

"Jesus Christ," the Irishman said. "You OK?"

"Not in the least bit."

Maps offered him a hand, pulling Garret to his feet and helped him into the ambulance.

The Irishman lit a match and tossed it into a puddle of fuel that traced back to the vehicle. Flames wicked up toward the sky, quickly consuming the truck.

Black smoke filled the sky in their rearview mirror. The Irishman drove with more care than usual, keeping his eyes peeled for another ambush. Would they have faced the same fate if they were still traveling together? No, they were fools. The Irishman shuddered those thoughts and focused on the road.

Maps treated Garret's fresh wounds in the back.

"Bastard got you good, huh, Garret?" the Irishman asked.

Garret winced as Maps dabbed a rubbing alcohol soaked cotton ball on his back.

"It was nothing I didn't deserve."

"Bullshit. That kid made his choice. You saved his life a few hours ago when you stupidly put yourself between our iron sights. I would've shot the asshole. If I have to hear you crying over him for the rest of this drive, I'll just get off here."

"They got ambushed by those things. Those aren't brain dead corpses like we once thought," Garret said.

"They got to be aliens using the dead as their shell," the Irishman said.

"Or it's the product of biowarfare," Maps added.

They continued to theorize back and forth for hours as they pushed forward, not daring to look back. Eventually, Maps and the Irishman switched seats. The gunshot wound in his foot was too aggravating for him to keep driving. Though it only took moments for the Irishman to aim his bitching at Maps.

"Stop hitting these goddamned potholes!" the brute yelled.

Maps tuned him out and continued driving Northeast, leaving the town of Celina as far behind as possible. After a solid five hours of driving, they were about 300 miles north, covering more ground than they had in days.

Maps pulled off the road and eased the ambulance into an empty church parking lot. They hadn't seen a single corpse or living soul since the wreckage. Maybe it was good luck, or they'd encountered enough bad luck for the universe to give them a break.

"Let me get the chili lime chips," the Irishman said.

Garret passed him the bag of chips and grabbed a can of green beans for himself. They ate mostly in silence, wolfing down their food like their life depended on it.

"How are you feeling?" the Irishman asked.

"Weird of you to ask, but I'm just a little sore."

"That thing fucking bit you!"

"So? It's just a bite. It didn't hurt as much as getting shot."

The Irishman's face turned red as he started yelling, "Just a bite? How fucking stupid are you? Have you ever seen a zombie movie in your life?"

Garret just sat dumbfounded as the Irishman continued his rant.

"What about you, Maps? You ever seen Night of the Living Dead?"

Maps shrugged.

"Both of you? I really can't believe this. Garret, you're a dead man walking."

"You're wrong," Garret said, not wanting to believe the Irishman's words.

"This is what's going to happen. You're going to get sick. I don't know when, but it's going to happen soon. And then you're going to die and turn into one of them."

"No, I'm not planning to die like that. Not after all the bullshit I've been through."

The Irishman just stared at him with a solemn look on his face. He tried to look Garret in his eyes, but couldn't, and turned away to stare at the white wall of the ambulance. "I should put a bullet in your brain now, before you die in the middle of the night and chew my face off."

"That won't happen. Are you basing all this off of a movie?" Garret asked.

"Well, a movie and some television."

Garret slammed his hand against the seat. "I'm going to make it home alive." He needed to believe his own words, but didn't.

After dinner they rode in silence for the rest of the evening, besides the loud snores coming from the Irishman. Eventually he woke up and switched roles with Maps, who quickly passed out in his stead. But Garret couldn't fall asleep, fearful that he wouldn't wake up again. He felt nauseous, but couldn't tell if it was from his dinner of green beans and chips, road-sickness, or if there really was an infection ravaging his system.

He stretched his neck to the side, trying to get a better look at the bite mark, but he could only see part of the bloodied bandage. Garret poked it with a finger and cringed as his pain receptors acknowledged his forceful prodding. The wound was irritated, but no worse than earlier. After Garret convinced himself that he wouldn't turn into a blood-thirsty monster, he passed out.

It felt like Garret had only been asleep for minutes, but when he woke he realized he must have slept hours because the sun was rising. Immediately, Garret touched his bite mark to make sure it hadn't just been part of his nightmares. He didn't feel any worse off. The swelling of the bite had actually gone down.

"Want me to take over driving for a bit?" Garret asked Maps, who responded by pointing to the bright orange fuel light. They were almost out of gas. "Where are we?"

"West Virginia, about 325 miles from Clearfield, Pennsylvania."

Garret smiled and sunk back down into the passenger chair. Another six hours and he'd be home. It surprised him how much ground they'd been able to cover overnight. Finally, a small stretch of good luck, no ambushes, blocked highways or impassable hordes of zombies. That was one of the reasons they preferred to move by foot, staying behind the cover of the trees and moving parallel to the road. They didn't have the convenience of covering hundreds of miles in a day, but they also didn't get ambushed like Cody and his family had been.

Maps killed the engine and parked the ambulance on the side of the two-lane road. Several yards to their north lay cars scattered about, on and off the road. It looked like there had been an unfortunate series of accidents, followed by further carnage.

Garret watched as Maps stepped out of the ambulance and onto the cool pavement with a hose wrapped around his shoulder and an empty gasoline jug in his hand. The slender man strolled over to a truck that had smashed straight into a tree. He ignored what little remained of two bodies in the front seats. The foul stench overpowered Garret, but didn't seem to faze Maps. The windshield and rear-view mirror were so caked with dried blood not a single ray of sunshine could shine through.

"Need a hand?" Garret asked what was essentially a rhetorical question.

Just as expected, Maps signaled back with a dismissive wave over his shoulder. Last time Garret helped siphon gas was back in Florida a week after he met the Irishman and Maps. He'd sucked a little too hard and got more than a mouthful of gasoline. Garret still remembered the disgusting taste and burn he felt in his throat, and he was sure Maps remembered him puking all over the jeep for a good five minutes after they'd refueled.

Garret heard the Irishman rustling around in the back of the ambulance. "Good morning, dickhead. You feeling hungover?"

"No, what about you? Feel like consuming brains? Does this look appetizing to you?" The Irishman peeled back his makeshift eye-patch to reveal a scabbed cavity where his eye used to be.

"No, you still look uglier than sin to me."

"Good," the Irishman said, sliding the patch back over his eye.

"So you've seen somebody turn into a zombie after getting bit?"

"Not exactly. Most people that I've seen bit, really just get torn apart like a piece of fried chicken. I've seen the way their dirty nails sink into a man's flesh and rip it open before they take a chunk out with their teeth. I guess you're lucky you didn't go out that way."

"So you're saying you don't know what the hell happens after someone gets bit? You've seen too many movies," Garret said.

The Irishman rolled his eyes. "There was a guy I knew back in Tampa that got bit."

"What happened to him?"

"I shot him in the face with a .22. Or no wait, maybe it was a .38. Fucking memory these days..." the Irishman trailed off.

Great. Another motivating speech from this asshole.

"So was he sick?"

"You know, I didn't exactly take his temperature. He got a chunk taken out of his shoulder, much like you. About an hour later he told me he felt woozy."

"Jesus Christ, so you shot him?"

"Well, he wasn't my fucking grandpa Garret. Just a coworker. And at the time, I thought maybe it was some airborne disease. So I wasn't really willing to share the same air with the guy."

Garret sighed.

"Come on Garret, he went quick. I did the 'look over there' trick," the Irishman said.

"Huh?"

"I pointed to the skyline and said look over there and then... Bang." The Irishman said it as if he'd done some noble act of charity.

"A real modern Mother Teresa, I see," Garret said, making the Irishman chuckle.

Despite the terrible story, a prickle of relief eased Garret's anxiety. His bite mark itched. A sign of healing.

Once Maps finished refueling the ambulance, they hit the road again.

They drove for about a mile before hitting a stretch of debris and abandoned cars. Moving at about a snail's pace, they weaved in between the wreckage. Dried blood smeared the windows of an overturned school bus. The ambulance crunched over broken glass and scraps of metal. Garret shifted his focus away from the sight of mangled school children and looked to the clear blue sky.

34

With a tap on his shoulder, Garret woke up. Maps pointed to a sign that read, "Welcome to Clearfield."

Unbelievable. For a moment Garret thought he must be dreaming. Familiar scenery passed by outside his passenger window. A warm feeling of nostalgia crept up Garret's spine. Clearfield looked like it'd been through hell, like the rest of the towns they passed through; sacked stores, burnt down buildings, wrecked cars in the street and an abundance of trash littered the streets. Yet he felt hope.

"Make a left here. Before we get to my house, I'd like to make a stop," Garret said.

"Oh, come on. I'm ready to drink this shot-up foot away," the Irishman piped up from the back of the ambulance.

Garret continued giving out directions until they pulled into a strip-mall parking lot. Wonderful memories came flooding back to Garret. Lee's Diner, a restaurant Garret and his wife frequented, sat across from the hardware, clothing and grocery stores. The phantom smell of freshly baked rolls made Garret salivate.

Garret's eyes welled up with tears, but he quickly rubbed them away. He didn't need anyone making some smart-ass comments. Before this nightmare started, this was where they shopped as a family.

"We're close to my house," Garret said with a sense of excitement.

"Why are we stopping?" the Irishman asked.

"I need something from the hardware store. And I figured we could loot the diner and grocery store while we're here."

"I'm not really up for a walk right now."

"Fine, stay in the car. Maps and I will be back soon."

The Irishman grumbled, but didn't argue. Maybe he thought Garret would find him some booze.

Only a few cars sat in the abandoned shopping square. The sun hid behind the clouds, casting long shadows across the pavement. Garret and Maps hopped out of the ambulance. It felt good to stretch their legs after sitting for several hours. As the blood rushed back into Garret's feet, he strolled up to Biggie Hardware and peered through a smashed window.

An eerie silence lingered through the store. Garret thought he saw a figure covered by shadows shift in the back of the store. Armed with a compound crossbow, Garret leaned over the broken glass, trying to get a better look.

"It's too dark," Garret said.

Maps shrugged. With a serrated knife in one hand, he opened the front door, triggering a set of bells. The loud jingle startled Garret. He followed close behind Maps. A guttural moan traveled through the darkness to the front of the shop. The sun waned behind them, not offering enough light to see clearly into the back aisles.

"We're not alone," Garret whispered.

Garret pulled a shopping cart from the cart bay and slowly pushed it down the aisle with Maps at his side. They cleared the store from left to right. In aisle four they stumbled upon a knocked over shelf of flashlights and batteries. Garret tore a flashlight from the packaging, flicked it on and tossed it to Maps. He filled the cart with extra batteries and a variety of flashlights while Maps provided cover.

Another eerie moan rose above the aisles. The noise put both Garret and Maps on their toes. The damn corpse must have heard them enter the store. As they continued through the shop, Garret and Maps added random items they thought would be useful. Soon their cart was filled with crowbars, a set of shovels, miscellaneous tools, and extra batteries.

"You finished?" Maps asked.

"Yeah, let's get out of here," Garret said.

Maps shined the flashlight through the shelves, scanning the other aisles for the source of noise. As they popped out of aisle 7 toward the front entrance, a foul scent filled Garret's nose. He looked down to see a corpse crawling toward them.

Garret recognized the zombie as Hendricks, the owner of the store. An exasperated sigh of disappointment escaped Garret's mouth. He had hoped the poor old man got out alive. Instead, he dragged his bloated body across the ground with his knuckles. The old man was missing the flesh from his legs. His bones scraped against the floor, making a noise that resembled nails scraping across a chalkboard.

With the compound bow raised to his shoulder, Garret took aim. The old man's sunken gray eyes bore into Garret. Hendricks was a good man. A man that deserved better than being picked apart and left to crawl around rotting in his own store. He'd been a pillar of the community, lived a good life and in the end died a horrible, meaningless death.

Garret wondered if Hendrick's wife Judy was still alive, or if she too suffered the same fate. Garret's thoughts kept him from pulling the trigger.Maps bent down and lodged his blade into the top of Hendrick's skull. The corpse went limp, Maps put his boot on his head and used the leverage to retrieve his blade.

A sick thought crossed Garret's mind. What if he got home and found his wife like this? The life missing from her eyes, mangled on the ground. The entire journey would have been pointless. Every life they lost on the way, wasted.

The sudden sound of emergency sirens snapped Garret out of his daze. Maps ran in front of him as Garret pushed the cart full of supplies out of the store.

Sirens blared loudly as the Irishman pulled up as close as possible to Biggie's Hardware. Fifty yards south of the parking lot, a swarm of zombies flooded to the center of town. Garret swung open the back door to the ambulance and with Map's help, they lifted the shopping cart into the back.

"Hurry the fuck up!" the Irishman yelled.

They climbed into the back, and before they could even close the door, the Irishman shoved his foot onto the accelerator. The ambulance peeled out of the town center, leaving the scent of burnt rubber behind them.

"I started seeing the hills sway. There are so many of those fuckers."

"They must have heard us or seen us," Garret said.

"Lucky I stayed in the car or we'd be dead right before the finish line."

35

THE ROSE RED sunset bled through the clouds, casting an orange tint over the Renner Barracks Cemetery. A cool summer breeze beat against the ambulance as it cruised through the graveyard.

The Irishman sighed as he brought the vehicle to a stop and asked, "A graveyard? Really, Garret? You came to pay respects to your grandma during a goddamn zombie apocalypse?"

"Shut up."

"Of all the places to stop. This is a bad idea," the Irishman said.

"Do you see any corpses walking around? I have to do this."

Despite the Irishman's grumbling, he killed the engine. "Go pay your respects fast and let's get the hell out of this creepy place."

A familiar sadness seeped into Garret, like how a drizzle of rain gradually dampens a shirt. It was a sadness that never really left. It hid inside Garret. For the past few months, it hadn't been as frequent. The aim of making it home to his wife dominated his thoughts, and for that he felt guilty.

"I'd appreciate it if you gave me a hand." Garret looked into the Irishman's remaining eye.

"OK, let's make it quick," he said.

They exited the ambulance. The quiet orchestra of insects chirped throughout the cemetery as Garret passed out shovels to Maps and the Irishman. Garret walked a well-acquainted route, weaving through gravestones. Lingering sadness engulfed him. He attempted to hold back a well of tears bubbling to the surface. He'd neglected this sorrow for too long. It came rushing back over him, a tidal wave of emotion.

The fading summer sunlight blanketed their backs. Headstones cast long shadows across the overgrown patches of grass. Garret stopped in front of a black granite headstone that read, "Kelsey Rittman, beloved daughter of Emily and Garret. April 16th, 2001 -- May 5th, 2012".

Garret pressed the shovel into the hard earth, tears streaming down his face. Together they dug in complete silence, flinging shovels full of dirt to their side. The sun faded from the skyline, leaving them to bask in the dusk. Garret let out a heavy sigh as the blade of his shovel scraped against the top of the cherry hardwood casket.

They stood over the tiny coffin. Memories of her illness, the funeral, and the lifeless look in his wife's eyes when they buried their baby girl came flooding back. The sheer amount of pain threatened to knock Garret to his knees. Like his lungs were full of nails, he struggled to breathe.

He tossed the shovel to the side of the freshly dug hole and knelt over the mahogany casket. Garret wiped the dirt off the top of the coffin. An anxious sense of dread filled Garret as he lay his head over the wood, pressing his ear against the casket.

"The fuck are you doing?" the Irishman asked.

"Shh," Maps said.

Garret listened for any noise, a sign of shuffling or scratching. He heard nothing. But the lack of sound failed to give Garret the sense of relief he was looking for.

With a quickened pulse, his heart throbbed painfully. Garret pulled at the latch pin. When it refused to give, Garret grabbed the shovel and thrust the blade into it, snapping it off. Still, the lid refused to open. Maps stepped down into the hole with Garret. Both he and Garret wedged the blades of their shovels between the casket's lid. Using the newfound leverage, they leaned into the handles of their shovels until a loud pop shook from the coffin.

Garret dropped his shovel to the side, bent over the lid, and pulled it open. His daughter's decayed body lay inside on top of the pillow padded fabric. She didn't resemble his baby.

"We can leave," Garret said, gently closing the lid.

The Irishman lowered his hand into the grave. Garret grabbed the muscled wrist, allowing the Irishman to help hoist him out of the hole. Maps followed closely behind, pulling himself out.

Garret had hoped for a sense of relief. The relief that his daughter wasn't trapped in a box for eternity, scraping at the ceiling of her coffin, moaning in pain and terror, engulfed in a never ending darkness. Instead of relief, it left him with an all-encompassing numbness. He thought of Cody's father, wondering if the boy's dad suffered the fate his beloved daughter avoided.

Maps patted Garret on the back, snapping him out of the spiraling train of thought. Together they shoveled dirt back into the grave until it looked like it was never disturbed.

"I had to know," Garret said.

Maps nodded in understanding. The Irishman said nothing. He turned his back to them as he limped forward, leading the way back to the ambulance. When they reached the vehicle, Garret swore he saw the Irishman wiping a tear from his eye.

36

DARKNESS SETTLED over Clearfield as they drove near the edge of town. The cover of night gave the familiar setting a sinister tone. They followed a winding road minutes from Garret's house.

"We're almost there," Garret said.

"Good, I need a stiff drink."

Maps drove cautiously, which Garret appreciated. Maybe he felt the same worry Garret did. A worry that they'd turn the corner only to be faced by a thousand corpses, ripping their goal from them in the home stretch.

At least the Irishman wasn't behind the wheel. Maps took each curve at a reasonable speed. The Irishman's driving would have Garret clutching onto the dash for dear life. Instead, he relaxed with the passenger side window rolled down. Cool summer wind breezed through the cab. It seemed the summer weather was at its tail's end.

Even now, Garret looked forward to the fall. He wished for his wife Emily to be OK. He'd give anything to share another moment with her on their deck, staring out into the woods, watching the leaves fall from the trees as they sipped hot tea.

"Please be home," Garret mumbled to himself.

"What was that?" Maps asked.

"Make the next right and then take the second left onto Oakview Road."

Butterflies surged through Garret's belly and into his throat. He wiped a nervous sweat from his brow as they turned into Oakview. Garret cradled his hands in his lap as he stared into the dashboard, afraid to look up and see what remained of his neighborhood.

"These are some nice houses," the Irishman said.

"Emily and I did OK. I'd like to think I was a halfway decent sales agent, and Emily wasn't a slouch either."

"You sold us on this idea three months ago when we were still in Miami," the Irishman said.

Garret laughed, "I thought you were going to kill me back in that mall."

The Irishman smiled and said, "Maps didn't want to waste the bullets."

"Thank God for that. Maps, turn onto this private road on the left. My house is at the end."

Tight masses of trees hugged the side of the narrow road, their canopies blocking the moonlight.

"What the hell did your wife do for a living? You must be loaded to have your own private drive," the Irishman said.

Before Garret could answer, Maps hit the brakes. The ambulance came to an abrupt stop in front of a sudden field of barbed razor wire. Their headlights illuminated the dried blood and torn flesh stuck to the barbs.

"What the fuck?" Garret grabbed a flashlight as he jumped out of the vehicle.

The razor wire stretched across the road in both directions, continuing into the forest brush. Garret flicked on a flashlight, traced the trail of barbed wire, following it into the woods. Maps carried a crossbow braced against his shoulder, and the Irishman closed his fists.

"Slow the fuck down. My foot's killing me," the Irishman said.

They relaxed their pace as they circled around the outer edges of the barbed wire. A groan traveled through the darkness.

"You guys hear that?" Garret asked.

Maps nodded as he overtook the lead, stepping in front of Garret, and signaled for him to get behind him. Garret fell back behind Maps and shined the flashlight across the sea of barbed wire. Several rows of the sharp steel coiled through the woods in what seemed like a never-ending loop. They continued following the path.

"We're only about 100 yards from the house. Looks like this is going to circle all the way around my backyard."

"Think your wife put this shit up?" the Irishman asked.

"It's possible, she's the survivalist type. Though I have to admit this is excessive, even for her."

Another guttural sound bounced through the woods. Garret swept the flashlight in an arc in front of him until the beam highlighted a tall figure tangled in the wire. The beaming flashlight revealed the giant of a corpse, dressed in ragged business attire. The steel defenses had stripped chunks of rotten flesh from its legs and torso. It fought against the wire, digging the barbs further into its ankles.

"Poor fucker," the Irishman said.

"There's got to be a way through."

They continued along the edge of the metal field until Garret spotted a faint light through lush tree canopies at the top of the hill. He shined the beam of light higher this time, sweeping over the barbed ocean.

"Look up there," Garret said. With the flashlight he highlighted two carbon steel lines strung over the field. Garret traced the lines with the light. The lines passed over their heads, leading to a tree behind them. "It's a zip line. Looks like that one is the exit. I think I know where we need to go." Without another word, Garret jogged along the outer edges of the barbed wire.

"Wait up," the Irishman complained.

Garret ignored him as he broke into a run, swinging the flashlight by his side. He circled up the hill, around the edge of his property line. A smile spread across his face as he reached his destination. He waited as Maps and the Irishman caught up with him, confusion painted on their faces.

"Christ, Garret, why the hell are you grinning like that?" the Irishman asked, breathless, with sweat rolling down his forehead.

Garret, still smiling, shined the light at the base of a thick tree trunk, lighting up the wooden boards nailed into its trunk. He guided the light up the makeshift ladder, revealing a tree house at the top. He'd nearly forgotten about the tree house he'd built for his daughter years ago. After her death, he never visited it again. Even the wonderful memories brought unwanted heaps of mental anguish.

They built it together. Well, Kelsey helped as much as she could for a ten-year-old. He let her help nail in the boards and decorate the interior of the tree house with stickers and acrylic paint. The look on her face when she climbed inside for the first time made all the effort more than worth it. He built it at the highest point on their property. The tree house overlooked their backyard and with a pair of binoculars, you could see it through the patio door leading to the deck.

Emily specifically wanted to see their daughter playing from the house or the deck. On cool summer nights they'd wave at her from the deck, signaling her to come down for dinner. Kelsey spent almost as much time in the tree house as she did inside their home.

"Garret, how did she die?" the Irishman asked.

"Cancer."

The disease snuffed out his daughter's life in a mere six months. They'd done everything they could to extend her life, chemotherapy, experimental treatments, but in the end nothing helped. Garret never forgave the universe from snatching the light of his life away. Years of therapy, support groups, and books on grief couldn't remedy his feelings of sorrow and loss.

"Tell me what really happened to Cody," Garret said.

"Fuck, not this again. Why are you bringing the dumb bastard up?" the Irishman asked.

"He tried to get me to leave with them. He begged me to go with him, to abandon you guys."

"Good thing you didn't or you wouldn't be standing here right now. Don't you realize we made it, Garret? You're fucking home. After three months of trawling through death and shit you made it, we made it," the Irishman said, slapping Garret on the back. "Don't sour this victory."

"Tell me what you said to him that afternoon. Cause you said something; he wasn't ready to leave like that. Something set him off," Garret said.

The Irishman crossed his arms and sighed before he said, "Cody wasn't like us. He was weak. Weak like you were when we first met. I don't even remember what I said that pissed him off. I was pretty wasted. All I remember was him crying about those cannibals we killed. I probably said something smart, and he swung at me. So I kicked his ass. His sister blew my foot off and we probably would've killed each other if you didn't intervene."

Garret pressed his palm to his forehead. "He was a good kid, man, couldn't you see that?"

"Good, gets you dead. We're just lucky he ate that ambush for us or we wouldn't be standing here now. Enough of this shit," the Irishman said, putting the conversation behind him as he climbed up the ladder to the tree house.

Garret waited as Maps followed the Irishman to the top. Finally, Garret joined them on the tiny deck on the tree house, taking in the view of his moonlight lit backyard. His eyes focused on the giant deck attached to the back of his house. It'd been one of the major selling points when they bought the house. He wished Emily would step into view.

"I don't see a harness or a trolley on this zip line," Maps said.

"Shit, you don't think..." The Irishman trailed off as looked over the sea of barbed wire under the lines.

"Of course, she doesn't want anyone having easy access over those defenses," Garret said.

Maps grabbed onto the line. He hooked his legs over the top and inter-locked the line between his feet. He pulled himself off the tree house's tiny platform, dangling twenty-five feet off the ground.

"Fuck, this has to be an eighty yard line. Garret, you couldn't grab any carabiners at the hardware store? I'm not a goddamn monkey like Maps."

Garret watched as Maps monkey crawled down the sagging zip line like it was second nature. The idea made Garret sick to his stomach. The thought of dropping into a bed of razor wire made him hesitate. It seemed the Irishman had similar reservations.

It took Maps less than five minutes to make it across the entire zip line. Once he made it to the end of the line, he released his grip and dropped a mere five feet to the ground. They could barely see the stick man waving his arms at them in the darkness.

"Fuck it," the Irishman said as he grabbed the line.

He hoisted himself over the zip line instead of hanging under it like Maps had. The line pressed into his belly as he hooked his feet under it, pressing the line into his good shin. He crawled head first over the rope like a commando. The Irishman took twice as long to make it to the end. Maps reached up to help lower the brute onto the ground.

"Guess it's my turn," Garret said.

Before leaving the platform, Garret grabbed onto the tense line, testing his grip. He sucked in a few deep breaths before hooking the taut steel line under his legs. He focused his eyes on the starry night sky and pretended he was only a few feet off the ground. The night air breezed underneath him as he crawled inch by inch toward his backyard.

Hot friction burned through his jeans as he dragged his legs across the coarse material. His hands blistered as he squeezed the line for dear life. For a moment he turned his head to check his progress, only to see he'd barely made it a quarter of the way down.

"Shit," Garret said as his grip weakened.

As he attempted to reposition his legs, the steel line slipped between them. The line bit into his hands as his legs swung underneath him. All of his weight hung from his wrists.

"What the fuck are you doing, Garret? Swing your legs back up there," the Irishman screamed.

Garret's wrists and shoulders ached as he clung to the hard line. He kicked his legs up, but they barely grazed it. Panic set in. Garret knew he was moments from falling if he couldn't relieve the pressure in his hands.

"Swing, you goddamn fool!" The Irishman's voice traveled across the yard, smacking Garret with his words.

This time Garret swung further back, harnessing the momentum to kick his legs forward. His left ankle landed over the line. The tension relaxed in his wrists as he hooked both legs back over the line, tighter than before. Determined not to fall to his death less than fifty yards from his own house, Garret pulled himself down the line with his eyes closed, focusing on each breath. A hand brushed against his back, startling him. He looked down to see Maps and the Irishman underneath him. He'd made it. Garret dropped, his heart still beating in his chest.

"Really smooth," the Irishman said.

"Good job," Maps added.

They stood underneath the massive deck, taking in the view of Garret's fortified backyard, while Garret caught his breath.

"Don't fucking move or I'll shoot all three of you in the back," a voice boomed from the deck above them.

Garret turned around, blinded by a shining beam of light.

"Garret?" the voice went soft.

The light lowered out of his face, revealing his wife Emily standing above them on the deck. Garret ran up the wooden steps towards her. She lowered the shotgun, dropping it on the patio table next to them. They embraced. Engulfed in the warmth of his wife's arms, Garret cried.

"You're alive," Garret said.

"Yes, and so are you," Emily echoed.

They kissed as they looked into each other's eyes. An immense sense of happiness and relief washed over Garret. Tears streamed down Emily's face as she cupped her husband's cheeks in her hands like he was a stray puppy that finally found its way home.

"I knew you weren't dead," Emily said, her voice cracking from emotion.

"Same," Garret whispered into her ear.

"You really stink, though." She laughed.

"Yeah, I know it's been a while since I've showered."

The Irishman and Maps walked up the steps, both sporting wide grins across their faces. They waited as Garret finished hugging his wife.

"Who are your friends?" Emily asked.

Garret laughed. "They're probably the only reason I'm here. But they don't really do names--"

The Irishman interrupted Garret, "The name's O'Brien, the skinny one is Micheal, but he doesn't talk much."

Maps greeted Emily with a wave of his hand. Emily ran over and hugged both of them. "Thank you so much for bringing my husband home to me."

She turned to Garret, "What's the slack-jawed look for?"

"Nothing," Garret said, "I'm just happy to see you."

The Irishman cleared his throat. "You going to give us a tour?"

AFTERWORD

Thank you for reading and following these characters on their journey. For questions or comments please email me at frankrobertson.author@gmail.com If you enjoyed the book or would like a sequel please consider leaving a review.

ABOUT THE AUTHOR

Frank Robertson is an emerging horror author and avid horror media fanatic. He resides in St. Louis, MO where he meticulously tracks every horror movie he's seen and book he's read. After consuming 1500 movies and hundreds of books he was finally inspired to produce his own terror packed novels.

When he's not writing he's watching 70's horror flicks, reading and petting his elderly cat.

Printed in Great Britain
by Amazon

23107430R10121